Cerberus

Cerberus

RAI BERZINS

GOOSE LANE

Published with the assistance of the Canada Council, 1993.

On the cover: "Dogface Boys' Picnic," by Sherry Grauer (1974-75), wire mesh, fibreglass putty, styrofoam, white glue, gauze, plaster, acrylic and aluminium paint, 91.4 x 254.0 x 304.8 cm. Reproduced with permission of the artist, courtesy of the National Gallery of Canada.
Book design by Julie Scriver.
Printed in Canada by The Tribune Press.

Canadian Cataloguing in Publication Data

Berzins, Andrew Rai, 1957-

Cerberus
ISBN 0-86492-166-7

I. Title.
PS8553.E79C47 1993   C813'.54   C93-098640-7
PR9199.3.B47C47 1993

Goose Lane Editions
469 King Street
Fredericton, New Brunswick
Canada E3B 1E5

To those who've been there
To Mary Ellen, with love, for the years

&

In memory of Arlo Goat Brakeman (1977-1993)
– dog of dogs

Contents

It'd gotten down to no-name Kraft Dinner a couple nights running so I thought what the hell. I got this idea — plan's too strong a word — to get some cash together and maybe try sculpture. Just construct stuff, stuff that doesn't work. There was this ad for security work, it was after five when I called but some guy answered, said come in tomorrow, so I did, bright and early.

The boss was this gouged-up brick shithouse with a brushcut and bad eyes but really on the level. His name was Cyril. It's funny with names, soon as he said *Just call me Cyril* I knew we'd get on fine. The pay was a couple cuts above minimum, nothing to write home about, and then there was the clothes. Grey pants, light blue shirt, royal blue blazer with company insignia, dark blue clip-on tie, and heavy-duty flashlight you could hook to your belt. Your belt you had to provide on your own, and the shoes, both of them had to be black. Cyril gave me a minute alone to suit up, to make sure I could live with the look. Enough guys he must've run into who couldn't. Right away there was a problem with the pants, none of them fit, they were all too long or wide. Cyril comes back, considers this a minute, pulls out a wad of bills, peels off two twenties, says *Here son get yourself some slacks,* then calls in another guard to take me shopping. It wasn't a thing of trust, he told me, just there were slacks and then there were slacks.

The guard, this Normund guy, comes strolling in, in uniform, cowboy boots, mirrored aviator shades, with a snub-
nose revolver replica belt buckle.

When I saw the buckle I wanted to laugh, but it hit me he
might have a real one in his locker. While Cyril explained the
situation, you couldn't tell because of the shades where
exactly Normund was looking. He stood there rocking from
spur to toe-cap, hands behind his back, crotch sticking out,
his neck super stiff like a whiplash victim. *No sweat*, he says,
interrupting, *good as done*. So we went to buy the slacks.

I'm not crazy about clothing stores, not saying Normund
was, but he knew how to shop. Right off he collared a salesman, told the guy we weren't there to dilly-dally, we had our
eye on something in grey, nothing fancy, just functional. The
salesman pointed out several styles, Normund chose one and
gave me the nod. I said sure, so that was fine, then Normund
spied some socks on special but I let him know I had lots at
home. *Your life*, he says with a sour face. We didn't talk the
whole way back.

They'd hired me on at ten in the morning but were so
stuck for bodies they had me start at three. The job was in
this luxury condominium highrise, just finished, smelling like
new carpet and fake air. We either sat at a desk in the lobby
or did patrols of The Premises. The suites were running half
a million a throw, they were empty but with locks we didn't
get the keys to, which seemed pretty strange seeing we were
the security. So we're just completing first rounds, Normund
was with me, he was doing a double, when he leaves me at
the monitors while he goes off to reheat some Big Macs in
the staff kitchen microwave. The guy at the desk goes off to
grab a piss, so I take a seat in the swivel chair. It feels like
you're flying a building. There's knobs and buttons and three
rows of TV screens, ceiling fish-eyes of corridors, blue and

empty and clean as hell. Like underwater, except without fish. I thought about eight hours staring at this, it was pretty depressing, when suddenly on one of the monitors an elevator opens and a woman comes out. This was my first actual sighting of the Princess but of course I didn't know it at the time. She comes right down the hall at the camera, she glides along like she's on a conveyer belt, like she's taken lessons how to walk, she's in this flashy man's-type suit, but it doesn't matter, you can tell what's underneath. And just when she's almost out of the picture her hand rises up across her front, stops on the left side just above where the heart'd be, and knuckles in at something. Now this could've all been innocent enough, bra-cup line adjustment, it's normal with women, but just before she's off the screen she glances up through a curl on her forehead and lets her eyelid close.

If that was a wink, I don't know, cause it's not like she wouldn't know someone was watching. You don't go closing your eye at a camera then pretend it was nothing, like a twitch or a sneeze. But that's as far as it got to go, she was gone and Normund comes back, secret sauce hanging off his moustache. His hair's near identical the colour of the sauce, but not quite, and it showed. I want to ask him about the woman, but first, to be fair, I point out the sauce. He wipes it off with the back of his hand, you'd think he was trying to wipe his total face off. Then he tells me to get off my ass.

It lands up we hardly talk the rest of shift, which is fine with me, or would've been, except how it comes out in other ways. We're doing the last exterior rounds, we're checking the windows on the promenade, when a couple women come strolling by in the opposite direction. Normund decides to check them out even though they weren't doing anything suspicious. First he beams them in the eyes, then lets the light wander down across their bodies. The one of them boy did she let him have it, the stuff she come out with'd peel the paint off walls. So she makes her point and they disappear and I'm there with Normund feeling sour in my gut. I let him know I think what he did was pretty uncalled for, but he responds they might've been anarchists, they might've had cans of spraypaint under their coats, he'd seen this program. They didn't look like anarchists to me, and I said so, and he said *exactly*, cause anarchists, the dangerous ones, were smart enough to dress like everybody else. South of here, he let me know, those women wouldn't have got off so easy. South of here he could've had a gun, and people don't mouth off when they're facing a gun. He'd seen some study in Time or *People*.

Late in shift we're sitting in the office, filling out our Incident Reports, when Normund sidles over with a couple of Cokes and puts one down beside me. *Coke adds life*, he says with a grin, but what I notice is how fucked his teeth are, sort of tortoise-shell, with half the side ones gone. He says *About earlier, that wasn't like an Incident, okay*? and I can't tell if he's trying to be helpful, or telling me my job, or covering his ass. It's not really something I want to get into, but he's got this lost look you can't just ignore. We get talking, about the job, about the city, the pros and cons, about the fastest route to work. It lands up we live in about the same area, and then before I even see it coming he's saying how we might as well head up together, up to the subway and I say okay. Anyhow I change my clothes, but Normund stays in uniform. He didn't have to, they provided us with lockers, but he wore his home every day. He liked being on the subway in uniform, people gave him room he said, and they did, though probably more because of his presence, or not quite presence, more just how he stared.

It was driving me crazy so I brought up the monitors, describing the woman I'd seen leave the elevator. *The Princess*, goes Normund, and his whole tone changed. At first I thought he was being sarcastic, calling someone a princess isn't usually a compliment. But Normund meant it, he'd decided she was royalty, and if she wasn't then she should've been. Apparently nobody knew her real name, but her job was handling Prospective Buyers. Normund wanted to ask her out, but he needed some kind of conversation starter. One way he thought would be great was to ask her if she'd traced her family tree, and if not why not, seeing how he for one would put down money her blood was blue. The right moment hadn't yet come along, but Normund felt it was just around the corner.

The next day I made sure to get in early. I had to sit desk and there was stuff I wasn't clear on, like bomb threat procedure and fire alarms. It lands up I'm standing in front of the change-room mirror, having a problem with my clip-on tie, when I notice this piece of paper taped to the wall. Newspaper, yellow with finger grease and spider shit, even so the date was only late last year. It had to do with that thing down in Kansas where security shot and killed these dogs that were screwing on the tarmac of an airport where the President's plane was soon to land. The guards were following orders — to make sure nothing moved. The dogs had already ignored one warning, a beating with somebody's welding gloves. The worry was the dogs might run in front of the plane, a Boeing 707, and that way cause an accident. Why exactly the article was up, to just point out the hazards of the job, or to stick by your buddies, it was anybody's guess. I wanted to know more about what they thought would happen if a dog ran into a 707. But that was all they said.

The next few days went by without incident, I mean incidents happened, but not like *Incidents*. They kept me on desk, it was a quirk in the schedule, and things between Normund and me'd cooled off. He must've noticed what I'd been doing with my tie, which was keeping the collar button undone and scrunching down my throat to cover the gap whenever Prospective Buyers went by, but he hadn't said a thing. He'd nod, I'd nod back, but even his nod had something pissed-off about it. Good odds he was probably mad I'd gotten such an easy first week, but the truth of it was I'd have jumped at a trade, desk for patrol, desk for anything, just to get a break from those buzzy blue screens.

It got to be Friday finally, and I sat at the desk scratching my neck, waiting for patrol to be by to relieve me. Four times in five days I'd had to shave, I'd got away with Thursday without nobody noticing, the thing with undoing my button had helped, but still my throat was putting up a fight, sprouting these pockets of pimple-type sores. The itch was something. So I'm there scratching when by mistake my finger hooks the tie and the clip-on clasp busts. First thing I'm thinking is flak from Normund, but the fact of the matter is it busted on the job. In the drawer there's some Band-Aids, so I go to work, rigging up this two-sided sticky knot deal. No sooner have I almost got the thing attached, than the elevator opens and the Princess comes out. She's not exactly in princess gear but she's no gutter queen either.

One thing I think some people forget is that video, no matter how good, is basically only moving dots. In real life there's body heat and slipstream and force fields. There's smell, like odours and bacon and perfume, and there's being able to *hear* someone breathe. Which the Princess is, she's breathing like a fiend, she's breathing like she just did stairs, which is weird since I saw her with my own two eyes come walking out of the elevator. Not that she's gasping, but just hard enough you have to go wow will you listen to that breathing. It's a sad sound, not exactly sick, but not like you'd want it coming out of you. We haven't made actual eye contact yet when it suddenly hits me — I don't know why — what if for example she's a bitch. What if she walks right by me oblivious, like we don't even share the same planet, never mind the room. All sorts of stuff starts pouring through my head. Before I know it I'm going all or nothing, I go and decide to ignore her first.

I stare at the screens like they're suddenly important, I hum a tune I don't even know the tune to, but in the end it doesn't matter, she makes a right where I thought she'd veer left, she heads off toward the promenade. The steps have just about disappeared when a little beeper goes off. I check the panel but nothing's lit up. Then the steps start coming back, the beeping stops, and I realize it's hers. One of those clip-on things for people on the go. She crosses the lobby calm cool collected, picks up a wallphone and dials a number. She's standing there turned sideways, waiting for an answer — you know when you lose control of your eyeballs? You can't get your act in gear to look somewhere else? It's weird, she's not even beautiful, not in any magazine way, but my mouth I feel it going gummy and stupid. Suddenly I wonder if some camera I don't know about is sitting there watching me watch her. It's one of the surest ways to drive yourself nuts, so I turn and look outside. She's talking about access and vestibules, cantilevers and interlocking brick. Just the way she says *interlocking brick*, it's no big mystery why she's in sales. The lobby looks out on this courtyard deal, which is where I'm looking when I notice the dog.

It's hard to know how long he's been there, standing by the window, trying to take a dump. He's stuck in this awkward squat position, trying to keep his balance till he gets some results. Every now and then he takes a little half-step, like in the hope it'll trigger the sphincter or whatever part in there's holding up the show. I'm thinking boy what the world won't deal you, even dogs, when all of a sudden Normund's at my elbow. He's got this thing for sneaking up on people, not that I was doing anything wrong, just that to Normund no half-assed security person should be able to get snuck up on.

He's standing there so goddam pleased with himself, when the phone receiver clicks down, and as he turns you see plain as day he didn't know anyone was back of *him*. Top of that, to have it be the Princess. She's scribbling something down on a pad, and Normund wheels back, his face gone white. Some guys get this crippled look when they find themselves without a plan. Normund's head clenches like a fist, then — who knows why — he turns back to face her, like he figured it was do or die. It was some situation, her coming past us, all of us round about the same age, us in our uniforms, her in her outfit, cashmere sweater, what looked like no bra, her making way more bucks than us, me feeling bent, Normund in love, her probably wishing guys weren't such animals — there's no point denying it, some staring was involved. I thought at first she might make a comment, her mouth was right on the verge of opening, but just then her glance dropped down to something that was happening below Normund's buckle. Just as quickly she looks away, but the damage was done, her heel lands wrong and she almost stumbles into us. To her credit she keeps on walking, holds her own until she's past, but then she stops. I don't know — the chest thing and all — I thought she might faint. What she does is stare out the window. Staring back in was the constipated dog.

He was still in his squat, still having problems, looking up with this grimace expression I'd call pretty rare in dogs. The

Princess stood there fascinated, like she was watching "Best of Wild Kingdom." Normund followed her look outside, then I looked at the Princess and she looked back at us, like in the hope we'd know what to do. Maybe Normund took that look and wound it totally inside out. Maybe just his sense of duty took over. Any rate, he fast got a plan, marched off to the maintenance closet, we heard a crack, then he comes back with the better part of a broomstick in his hand. I don't know why he felt he had to break the broom-part off, maybe just the heat of the battle, but anyhow he continues off past us out the door to the courtyard.

You hear people say how dogs know what's happening? I got my doubts. This one thought Normund was coming to the rescue, when what the dog got, once Normund had cornered him, was a vicious wallop across the ass. The dog didn't even bother to yelp, but looked up at him with these gooey eyes, which sat even worse with Normund, who followed up with a round of blows, most of them landing square across the skinny haunches. The dog must've finally got the idea the guy in the uniform was not a friend. He ducked one pretty high-velocity swing and got himself safely out of reach. No sooner's he clear than his bowels must've shifted into overdrive. Out comes a string of dry hard turds, like he'd been saving up for a week, odd stuff like blackened figs. He moved off further, then turned to face Normund, the turds in a cluster some halfway between them. Then the dog lit up with a howl, the sorriest sound you'd ever want to hear, while Normund stared back, trying to work out protocol. Seemed to me we were nearing an Incident. Several people yell over at him, we couldn't make out what they were saying, but there wasn't much doubt they were siding with the dog. Normund looks up at them, not like he was listening, but like he was figuring where to go from there.

Finally he turned and his eyes met mine. I thought of what he'd said about south of here, that south of here he'd have had a gun. Then he could've shot the dog, turned around with the gun in his hand, and seen what those civilians had to say. Kansas got nothing on anywhere else, providing you got the required equipment — which, in our case, Normund didn't. Instead, he dropped the broomstick where he stood, looked down at the turds, then came back inside.

He goes right past the Princess like she's not even there, he stops at my desk, slouches against it, and draws in this long wheezy breath. *Dog shit on the walk*, he goes, matter-of-fact, like it's routine, but his voice is thin like they siphoned off the person, like there's nobody home. *There's a shovel in the closet*, he adds, then looks from my face to my throat to my tie. His eyes cloud over looking at the tie, lying there with its busted clip, its Band-Aids, on the desk. There's things there's no point trying to explain. I got up, took off my jacket, and laid it down beside the tie. The Princess stood right where she'd been, her knee had a wobble but that was it. I walked around the desk, brushed past Normund, and headed toward the outside door. Both of them turned to watch me go. I know cause I could see it all, the three of us, the whole she-bang, in this monster mirror that covered one wall. Normund's forehead doing an accordion, the Princess knuckling that spot on her chest. Me trying to wipe off this silly grin, and once I did I turned back to face them, to give them both a chance to talk, but we must've all realized there was nothing to say. It was weird, it was almost like a friendly moment, but I didn't want to push it so I went out the door.

The dog was gone, the sun was out, so I headed back to the office. Cyril wasn't in so I left a note. I just said I wasn't cut out for the job and left it at that, there wasn't much point. Cyril, bless his brushcut, paid me through for one whole week. It was only a question of thirty extra bucks but thirty bucks is thirty bucks. I cashed the cheque, went down to the pound and checked out the dogs, I'd been meaning to. There was this one, this spooky calm part-Malamute, part-something else. The other dogs were acting like dogs, licking their crotches or barking or stuff, but it stood still, checking me out. I bent down and it wandered over. It licked my fingers through the fence. One eye was blue and one was brown. I tried to think of a name — to call it — but my mind went blank. Sort of entirely.

Very same day I got a job doing demolitions. Factories mostly, and out-of-date stores. It's not the most creative work, but it's working with space, and that's a start. I don't have to shave or wear a tie. The boss says we're changing the face of the city. One thing's for sure — it beats beating dogs.

ZIEMAN BESIEGED ▪

The geriatric unit is quieter than most, the sleep is deeper, but the gas is worse. Zieman, waking, scrapes the crust from his tear ducts, puts down the bedrail, and heads off down the hall. He nods to Floyd, who is returning from the washroom, half a pyjama leg soggy and clinging.

"Sons of bitches," says Floyd. "The bastards."

Zieman does not contend the issue. He rams the washroom door with a borrowed cane, then steps from the lino onto tiles flypaperish with settled urine mist. He tugs out his own weathered faucet, relaxes and listens, with eyes closed, till he hears the liquid drum across the seat.

A knock on the door and a female voice: "Mr. Zieman, raise the seat."

"Seat?"

"The one you're urinating on."

He makes the adjustment, and fluid hits fluid, and everybody's happy, and the steps go off. The last few drops he flicks to the wind.

The breakfast menu offers varnished waffles, watery eggs with two strands bacon, coffee or tea, toast, marmalade, and juice. Zieman is new and so bears watching. Beside him sits Floyd, not convinced how to eat, his chin, like a jerky pendulum, seemingly intent on swinging free of the face. The nurse in attendance assists with utensils.

Zieman sponges up some crumbs with a licked thumb, looks up, and finds Murray (female) and Beldam (male) staring.

"For juicier oranges," Zieman says evenly, "submerge in hot water for fifteen minutes. This gives twice the amount of juice."

Murray and Beldam find elsewhere to look and, after a minute, leave.

"Bastards," says Floyd, with suspicion, at the eggs.

"Who is that man and why is he here?" Murray asks her nurse for the day.

"For treatment or assessment, like everyone else. His name is Mr. Zieman."

"Which is it?" says Beldam. "Treatment or assessment?"

"That's really his business, don't you think, Mr. Beldam?"

"He has a look about him," says Murray.

Across the room Zieman hovers at the nursing station window, requesting cigarettes. He is told his smoking will be monitored, given the staff's unfamiliarity with him. In fact (and unsaid), it has more to do with the circumstances of his arrival: a court order for psychiatric assessment with regard to the issue of competence. A fire in Zieman's building had begun in his room. Zieman was vague. Charges were waived on the understanding that he'd be clinically assessed. For the time being he's allowed to smoke, but in the lounge, in full view of staff.

Maintenance men are repairing a window through which someone tried to put the couch. Zieman watches them touching up the trim, or what would appear to be touching up the trim. It's hard to distinguish the painter from the brush, the brush from the trim, the trim from the window, especially

with cataracts. He squints, and a painter, assuming he's wink-
ing, winks back in the way of rapport.

"Soften old brushes by soaking in hot vinegar, then wash
in warm soapy water," says Zieman. "Add fabric softener to
keep the brushes pliable. For small touch-ups, use cotton swabs."
He sighs, then takes a deep inhalation.

"Nosy Parker," Murray says, with peeved breath.

Beldam glares.

The Lounge Occupation, in late-morning phase, consists of
Beldam, Murray, Paz (male), Daumier (female), Knapp (male),
and Major Drinkwater Junior (female). The topic — in hushed
tones — is Zieman's background.

"So — what — *German*?" Beldam toils.

"And if so?" asks Knapp.

"Just interested," says Beldam. "Something the matter with
that?"

"There's a *manner*," notes Murray, meaning Zieman's.

Down the hall the telephone rings.

"We all have manners," Beldam counter-notes.

"Some less than others," mutters Paz.

"That's not — oh heavens!" says Murray, exasperated.

The telephone stops on the second ring.

"Baltic," states Knapp. "Baltic or Balkan."

"*Balkan*?" Beldam leaps several octaves.

"Balkan," says Knapp, pleasant, dismissive.

"Speak of the devil," says Murray in an undertone, facing
the corridor down which Zieman comes.

"Telephone, a . . . Mr. Bedlam?"

"*Beldam*," Beldam is quick to make clear.

"No points there, I'm afraid," says Zieman.

Beldam wavers, wondering if he's been insulted.

"Who's for caca?" Major Drinkwater Junior proposes, buoyant for reasons very much her own.

From the lunch menu of chile con carne, braised oxtails, cream of mushroom soup, French fries, and plums, Zieman has selected the latter three. Placing the dishes triangularly before him, the fries at the apex furthest away, he sits and gauges the composition.

Something with the potatoes is wrong. He plucks from the mound two or three offending fries and, without much interest, puts them in his mouth. He glances up and catches Beldam staring. Beldam returns his attention to his own plate, and Zieman his to the arrangement.

"Dried-out shoes — if that's your problem — can be restored by rubbing a piece of raw potato on the leather," Zieman says, then looks up.

"French fries wouldn't do?" returns Beldam.

"No. Not as I understand it."

"Not as he understands it!"

"No."

The others calmly continue with their meal, while Zieman takes out a cigarette, places it on his lip, and pauses. Beldam turns to the No Smoking sign, soaks up its authority like bread in soup, then turns back on Zieman his fortified glower. Zieman has made no move to light up, so Beldam warily returns to his soup.

"He'll rue the day," he murmurs to Murray, who indicates, by way of pointed glance, that one does not speak with one's mouth full.

Beldam's spoonings proceed in silence, interspersed with less than furtive glances in Zieman's direction. One of these, prolonged by Zieman's fumbling with something in his lap, throws off Beldam's delicate rhythm, and a spoonful of soup takes a detour down his chin. He snatches up a napkin, but before he's decent a flash goes off from across the table.

Zieman, an Instamatic camera in his hands, is peering down at the plate arrangement.

Beldam wipes his chin clean, stands and points a quivering finger: "That's a camera! Cameras aren't allowed!"

"Neither, I'd think, are outbursts," says Zieman.

"There's a hospital rule," says a nurse's aide.

Zieman nods, and puts the camera away. He sits, takes his spoon, and cautiously tests the stiffening surface of the soup.

Nathan Veigle, the assigned psychiatrist, enters his office with a half-finished lunch of chicken wings to find Zieman waiting.

"Mr. Zieman." Veigle offers his hand.

Zieman neither turns nor stands, remaining instead with eyes closed, sifting through the smells in the room. "No offense."

"None taken," says Veigle. He shuffles through some papers and brings up Zieman's file. "Excuse the delay. We had a hectic morning."

"Perhaps they wouldn't miss them."

"I'm sorry?"

"The chickens. If they just removed the wings, let the chickens carry on . . . "

Veigle looks up to find Zieman looking down. "Yes," he says, and scribbles briefly. Unreliable historians pose problems, unless well-documented on previous admissions. To the hospital's knowledge, Zieman had none. Sodium amytal might be in order, hypnosis — but these would require consent.

"As for you, as opposed to the chickens ... " A smile. "The reason we're here today ... "

"Luck of the draw." Zieman sighs. "There, but for the grace of God ... "

"The court order ... "

"Kangaroo court."

"You *are* aware of why you're here?"

"Assessment, with regard to fire-hazardousness."

"Uhn-huhnnn, now is that how you'd view yourself? Could you tell me how you'd view yourself?"

Zieman looks about the room (Veigle tracking as best he can): at the cacti, the Van Gogh print, the framed credentials, the Rubik's cube, the tropical postcards, the departmental memos, the "Order of the Good Time" diploma, the Escher calender, the files, the textbooks ...

"You take a man ... driving a Pontiac. The man doesn't matter much ... who the man is. The car though ... the Pontiac ... named for a small town in Michigan ... where the car is made." He squints. "I could be wrong on this ... let's say for the sake of argument ... there is the car named after the town, the town named after the Indian, the Indian chieftain, the fellow — Pontiac — who held the British under siege ... Detroit, seventeen-something ... seven ... Seven Years' War ... for several months. The British held out, defeated the French, and then in turn were defeated by the Americans. Pontiac was dead. Cars came along. And, with the cars, the naming of cars. The name Pontiac becomes a car. A man who tried to defeat a city, a city which went on to become the hub of the largest automotive empire in the world, the man is remembered as a car. To answer your question, I don't see it matters ... how I view myself."

Veigle hunches, his hand on his chin, two fingers propping

up the lip. Zieman, in spite of his damaged sight, can make out chicken-wing sediment caught between the teeth.

"You sense some special affinity?"

Zieman offers a neutral shrug, and mutely asks for a cigarette.

The doctor hesitates, then complies, holding forth his Association lighter, out of which the blue oval pops and flutters beneath Zieman's parched blue eyes. He's burned up a third of the cigarette before Veigle's hand jerks from the heat, and he notices Zieman likewise oblivious.

"The British are history," Zieman says darkly.

"Manage a walk, Lynn, later perhaps?"

"Pay attention or there's no sense playing."

Beldam basks in the reprimand. Murray lays down a nine-card run. They are playing rummy, Murray's rules, Murray cleaning up.

Knapp, nearby, decides it's time for his joke, pulls himself together, and stands. "I'm going to take my Knapp," he announces, bows, and gracefully staggers off.

Today his delivery is cleaner than usual, and the group, but for Beldam, is quietly amused. The latter, holding grudges like life preservers, wishes him only a quiet death.

"Checkmate," comes a voice from behind them.

Murray declines to acknowledge the intrusion, but Beldam feels obliged.

"Thinks we're playing chess of all things! Here we are playing rummy, and he thinks it's chess. Maybe some people should think before they speak."

"Clive, don't encourage him."

"I'm not. I'm giving some overdue advice."

Zieman takes a position between them, and mimes the action of reeling in a fish. Beldam wheels to confront his antagonist. Instead, his glance meets Zieman's crotch.

"Your zipper, Mr. Zieman!"

"Your mouth, Mr. Beldam."

"*Must* you?" snaps Murray, to Beldam's aid.

"For stuck zippers," Zieman replies, "rub soap up and down to lubricate the teeth." He turns, goes and takes a seat on the couch. "Might I borrow a cigarette?" he asks of Daumier, snug on his left.

"Butter wouldn't melt in his mouth," Murray mutters, with evident disgust.

"His cigarettes are monitored," Beldam warns.

"Trying to get my goat," explains Zieman. "Seems to think I have one."

Daumier smiles, as does Paz, and offers him her pack.

Supper consists of veal scaloppine, waxed beans, cauliflower, sautéed potatoes, and rice-raisin pudding.

"Fish," says Paz. "Today's our day for fish."

The server makes clear the limits of his duty.

Paz takes vegetables and moves to his table.

"Picky, picky . . . " Beldam taunts.

"Would you like to *know* about veal?" offers Paz.

"Meat's meat," says Beldam routinely.

"To *you*," says Paz before savaging a bean.

Beldam manages the sense to leave well enough alone.

"Not so bad were it just the cold," Murray observes, of the storm outside.

"Wind that worries me," says Beldam, taking his seat beside her.

"When will weather wipe us off the map?" muses Knapp,

somewhat out of sorts as he often is after being too abruptly roused for supper.

"They shouldn't let him nap," concludes Beldam.

Zieman enters the dining room as the server is closing, declines a plate, takes from his carry-all a compact blender, and plugs it into the wall. From atop the fridge he takes some bananas, from inside the fridge a raw egg, a couple cups milk, from his pocket some chocolate, places the lot in a quart-size container, and blends it to a froth. Proceeding to his seat beside Floyd he pours two glasses and takes one up. "Out of house and into home," he says like a sadly occasioned toast.

Floyd takes his glass and downs the contents.

"What on earth . . . " Murray protests, imagination laying to waste her tongue.

"A Zieman Mixer," Zieman announces.

"First-rate," says Floyd through smacking, foamed lips.

"Rabid," says Beldam.

But no one pays him any attention. They are watching Floyd, his broad messy jaw, and the mouth from which, for the first time in memory, words have emerged not yoked to curses.

The student psychologist wants Zieman's thinking on people in glass houses throwing stones.

"Permanent residents?"

"Whatever comes to mind."

Zieman is silent well into a minute, before he clears his throat to begin.

"Given the uh . . . *climate*'s the best word . . . given that, the climate, it would . . . seem uh . . . *sensible* . . . sensible to not throw stones. Break a window — or wall, seeing the walls too . . . the walls would be glass. Have to depend . . .

thickness of glass . . . Griffith criterion for crack propogation
. . ."

The young man scans his list of proverbs.

"One could . . . hypothetically . . . get out of the house,
throw away from the house, which it would seem would
diminish the risk. Unless the neighbour had a glass house
too. You might ask yourself why you're throwing stones in
the first place, or why . . . why in the world a glass house?"

The young man studies him.

"If you'll excuse me I'm feeling nauseous," Zieman apo-
logizes, and goes.

"The chill, that's half the battle," says Beldam, at a standstill
in his crossword.

"Penetrates." Murray flips a card in solitaire.

"Goes right through you," Beldam confirms.

"I don't require paraphrase, thank you," says Murray.

Zieman sidles into the lounge, looking for what he might
have done with Knapp's cane.

Beldam faintly shudders with internal combustions.

"Deal me in," says Zieman, probing nearby.

"It's solitaire," says Beldam. "Besides, I'm next."

"Two-hand."

Beldam shakes his head.

Zieman takes a seat at a table where tea and a plate of cookies
are laid out for evening snack, minutes away.

Murray completes her game with a sigh.

"Are you a euchre man, Mr. Zieman?" Paz inquires from
across the lounge.

"A *euchre-man*." Zieman gives it some thought.

"I've heard it all," Beldam groans, stands, then pauses while his bowels adapt. "Hold the cards, will you, Lynn? Business before pleasure."

"Raise the seat," says Zieman as he passes.

"Tell that to your Floyd!" barks Beldam, continuing off down the hall.

"Faculties intact?" ventures Zieman. Murray doesn't return his glance. He reaches for the teapot to pour himself a cup.

Murray's thinking she keeps to herself, or so she supposes, unaware of the agitation of her delicate hands shuffling cards like nobody's business.

"Casino born," says Zieman, impressed.

"*What*?" Murray stiffens.

But Zieman's attention has already wandered, so much so that he overpours his tea and continues pouring.

Murray watches the brown pool widen, reach the edge, and spill over to his lap. Zieman takes notice, with a grimace and a start.

"Where's the nurse?" Murray demands. "He's worse than a child," as though she's just noticed.

Paz comes over with paper towels and lays them on the spill.

"He has more sight than he's willing to admit," says Murray, seeking some vindication in the prospect of his long-term deceit.

Zieman stares down at the dark stain spanning his crotch like a threat of things to come.

Beldam whistles, then makes his entrance, holding out a coupon-bonanza envelope. "Look what I found."

But no one else seems to fathom its significance.

"Handy Household Hints!" says Beldam. "It was on his desk, all those things he's been saying . . . the paint brushes

and oranges and what to do with stiff shoes . . . here on the
envelope — *he took it all from here!*"

"What were you doing in his room?" asks Paz.

Beldam looks at Paz like he's from another planet, snorts,
and looks about for allies. All eyes are on him but none very
warm.

It's too much for Murray — "I'll be in my room . . . " —
her voice trailing off as she rises, then goes.

Beldam sits to avoid collapse, the cards spread before him.

"Euchre-man, no reason why not," says Zieman, weary
but willing to try.

Paz takes a seat and shuffles the deck.

Everyone has gone to sleep, except for the night staff, and
Zieman in his room. Ballasted with blankets, sitting up in
bed, he handles his cameras, he shifts them in his hands.
There are voices in the air-vent, voices in the walls, and below
them all the strange planet moving.

He picks up a screw-mount, a bayonet, compares them by
weight, girth, ease of rotation. He puts them down and picks
up a body, presses the cool metal flush to his cheek. He sets
the shutter at a full second, cocks the lever, holds it to his
temple, breathes out, and trips the release.

The mouth in the camera clucks its tongue.

He glances across at the photo on the desk, a photo he
knows so well he's no longer sure whether he sees or has it
memorized — young people in a birch-wood clearing, phantoms in the half-light, and, in the foreground, in black beret
and leaning on a bicycle, the likeness of Zieman half a century ago.

When the staff come by on their night rounds, he peers back at them from the edge of his forest. What do they expect — open arms?

Pontiac was done in by one of his own.

And still it's hours till dawn.

SEA OF TRANQUILITY

Hardly sees it coming. Suddenly it's here. Night of the elves, mistletoe, a far-off sun exploding millions of years ago, the long slow telegram singing through space, flicker in the dark then blaze, dissipating into code.

Thirty-three and a week, Rudy. Winter baby. Looking up, three days off the darkest night. Nearly falls on the way in, service ramp, the rain glazing to hazard undetected till it's seconds too late. Caught himself, got an elbow out, grabbed a dangling maple bough and broke the fall. Spilled beans, spilled brains. Bruises his hip, in the end, is all. Limps in. Joints in their own slow slide out of kilter, another year passing.

Sea of Tranquility. There'd be a place.

Thinks of a friend who swears she saw, on the first televised transmission from the Moon, reflected in the glass of Neil Armstrong's face-shield, a figure — *conquistador* — looking around.

Security shout to lend them a hand, hold down a woman in Emerge for a needle. Paraldehyde. Robot cum. Smell the stuff coming yards away, creature sneaking up your nostrils, halfway to your brain lays eggs. Works though, is why they use it, it drops the average person like a rock. Excepting people like the woman in this case, who probably already had done regimens of every conceivable every available kick to the head that pharmacology's invented. They got her down, got her horizontal, but not before she managed to claw a couple strips off an arm or two. One young guy holding off his hysteria, eighteen maybe, no good the English, eyes in his head rolling like marbles, sweat breaking out across his brow, likely stories he's heard of AIDS and Hep-B and where in hell those fingernails have been, the scalp cells and fecal matter and nosepickings and eyeball discharge, just as a nurse appears with gloves, five-prong condoms, latex taut. Thinks of a patient, compulsive, who brought in his own rubber gloves with which to jerk off, so as not to infect himself . . .

Security boys, the sorry mothers, are not union, are not contractually *obliged* to hold down a bleeding person, have no details, only rumours, the hospital lax in restricting their role. Rudy takes over from the scratched kid, who rushes off to get sterilized. Rudy with ten years holding down slashed and punctured limbs, torsos, throats, long before gloves, behavioural screening, bio-hazard protocol, ten-foot poles. Thinks now and then about piss in the eye from a guy who sometime later died, or wiping others' blood from a hangnail. Foreign bodies in the stream.

Meanwhile the woman is screaming she's God, from Memphis, intends to sue their asses. The only accent's from disengaged dentures. She takes twenty minutes to hit glass pasture, lies there limp, spittle on her lip. *The yet unburied bones of God . . .*

Rudy lands in Psychosomatic, half the place empty, out on pass. He's there for coverage, nothing more. Winds up underlining dates in patients' charts with bright red pencil, the charts going back six seven months, but the doctors like the dates underlined, says the nurse, they like their coffee hot. He volunteers to do the rounds, only four bodies, but one anorexic they have to check to make sure is asleep and not doing sit-ups in bed in the dark. On the bedside table of a sleeping bulimic he finds a *Playboy* and glances through. Year-end review. He's at Miss May in the dim glow of the baseboard lights when the call comes — purple code, Crisis. Folds the flesh back into the pages, the bulimic turns and opens an eye, but, before he can focus, Rudy is gone, a thin trail of atoms, a figment, or less.

The woman from Memphis stands in a washer tucked into an alcove near the Crisis unit washrooms, threatening to turn it on. She calls for a lie detector test, has quarters galore, claims no next of kin. In the minute someone left her alone, she managed to barricade the door, two-panel swing type like in saloons, with a knotted sheet and heavy mop handle.

"I shall wash the sins from my loins!" she shouts. "To death at least I shall go cleansed!"

They lure her out with a cigarette, coffee, and an ice cream sundae. She wants all microphones removed from her room, the country returned to an agrarian society, free local telephone, a ban on exhaust. Everyone agrees they'll do what they can. *In the still of the night* . . . so much seems possible.

Once she's out, the only discussion is over which buttock was done last. Both sites seem tender, but the nurse, fairly novice, is worried by the lack of sufficient flesh elsewhere. The woman from Memphis says go ahead — *the ass* — and the nurse sincerely thanks her for her understanding. The shot goes fine and soon the woman from Memphis is drifting through *Vogue*s on her bed. Rudy sits in a chair in the hall directly across from her doorway. On the hallway wall are plasticized art prints, left of the door some lillies by Monet, right of it fruit by Cézanne. The hallway light is too low for reading. The pictures are pretty, a century old. Always Monet or Cézanne or Seurat, sometimes Van Gogh, depending. Rarely Matisse. Never Toulouse-Lautrec, Munch, Klimt, Gauguin. Pleasant impressionists, then a leap to recent high realism, neo-nouveau: flowers, teacups, cats, spoons. Rarely Colville, rarely Pratt. Never an expressionist, Dadaist, surrealist, cubist, actionist, popist, post-modernist. Never Bosch, occasionally Brueghel, sometimes Renoir, never Goya. Never never Géricault. Now and then the Group of Seven. Once, perhaps by mistake, a Rothko.

"Speak not at all, but carry a curse."

The woman from Memphis. Rudy looks over to where she slouches on the bed, a *Vogue* in her lap, her head tilted up, throat exposed, a brilliant white column. Her gaze travels out the window, through shrubbery, across the lawn, over the hedge, the spiked fence, the street, the power lines, up past the buildings, into sky, in the middle of which hangs the moon. She snaps her fingers and points to the light switch. Rudy gets up and darkens the room. Moonlight streams in, caging the bed.

"Women like me, that's where we go." Her voice is softer than the light. "No man in the moon. No cheese, no cows. Moon's not huge, but it's bigger than Europe. Think it'd be spacious. Not so, my friend. Nice view though. Cliffs to jump from. Land on your face as long as you desire." She turns and looks directly at Rudy, her face filmy, scoured with threads of shadow. "After we die?"

Rudy swallows, thinking it a question. But the woman from Memphis turns back to the moon. Her eyelids waver and gradually fall. It's then he notices his throat gone dry. Air in the place like a mausoleum's, add to that the beers before work. The other aide — Paul — relieves him. Rudy goes to the kitchen fridge, looks for juice but finds only prune, has a glass, then a second, is starting a third when he wonders does he really want his ass leaking coleslaw and gyros beef till dawn?

His hour off is ending when he hears a confrontation filtering down the hall from Memphis. The nurse looks up from a chart and reminds him the woman has no meds for another hour. Rudy gets a coffee and goes.

Paul is at the door, in the armchair, his feet propped high against the doorjamb. The woman from Memphis stands in the furthest corner of the room, balanced on one foot, her arms locked across her chest, the ungrounded foot twisting like the head of a snake. She is groaning something through her teeth and staring at Paul who is reading *Sports Illustrated*.

"She's all yours," he says and swings his body out into the hall in one fluid motion.

Rudy takes the seat, and the magazine. It's the college football preview which he scans without interest.

"Man should be shot."

Rudy looks up.

Her free foot is rhythmically stroking her calf. "I can't be more specific," almost an apology.

They've coexisted in silence for fifteen minutes when Rudy feels himself break from a trance. She's squatting on the window ledge three feet off the floor, working away at a screw in the frame.

"What're you doing?"

"Leaving."

"Get down."

Rudy approaches, and she swings out at him. He grabs her wrist and firmly pulls her from her perch. She kicks back and

up with her heel, but he closes his knees, locking the foot before it can reach its target. It's a taut shuffle-dance the
distance to the bed, but he gets her there and holds her.

"Don't be a motherfucker," she says, calmly, like advice.
"Don't tamper with forces beyond your comprehension."

After a moment he relaxes his grip, eases up and away
from her. He's no sooner back in his chair than she's up again
on the windowsill ledge. Again he approaches, this time
more cautiously, and holds out a hand for her to take.

"Stay the night. Talk to your doctor tomorrow."

"Easy for you to say. Forked tongue and all."

He reaches further and she kicks out at him, loses her balance and starts to fall. He catches her shoulders and steers
her back to the bed, at which time she tries to bite his arm.
Her teeth lock, but only snare the heavy corduroy of his
sleeve. He tugs his arm free and with it come her teeth, the
top six and their anchor-plate. The denture falls onto the
blanket between them. Rudy, in surprise and unexpected re-
vulsion, pulls away and returns to his chair. The woman stays
where she is on the bed. He takes the magazine and pretends
to read, mouthing the words, as though this might convince
her. It doesn't. The denture strikes the wall a couple of inches
inside the doorjamb, the teeth cracking free and rebounding
back across the floor, a burst of queer chatter. He counts to
five, looks up and sees her sitting quietly, hands folded,
where she was. He picks up the plate, not far from his feet,
rinses it off in her alcove-sink, and places it on a cloth on her
table. She does not move. He picks up two of the teeth, the
only ones he can find without a search, and places them also
on the cloth. He backs to his seat, sits, crosses his arms. Fifteen minutes? ten? twenty? before relief, before someone else's
turn.

"*Stay the night,*" she says with the thinnest, smallest of laughs. "Till death do us part."

She lies back and soon is asleep, and Rudy relaxes, feels his tissues, muscles, bones, twisting down into lump camaraderie with the chair.

He's scribbled the rudimentary hour synopsis, *affect,* sleeping pattern, behaviour . . . short addendum on the broken denture, when he suddenly wonders about her faith. He goes to the front of the chart, the admission notes, but finds, of course, the briefest of outlines. Everything that interests him — *see old chart.* Since her midnight admission, however, the old chart has surfaced, from two years previous. Carole ____, 36, bipolar, separated, with a twenty-year-old son. Occupation: architectural rendering artist (owns own firm). Religion: other.

He scans through Medical History and finds a reference to the teeth, lost due to vitamin deficiency during her teenage pregnancy.

It does not say if she got to keep her son.

When he returns for his last hour of sitting, she's still asleep, in fetal position, unblanketed on the bed. Paul too is drifting, and wakes with a start. His foot knocks over a can of pop which clatters, frothing, across the tile. Carole stirs but does not wake. She stretches, turns, and settles on her back, her arms tangled above her head.

Paul raises a groggy brow, mutters "lucky stiff," then goes.

Rudy can't decide if he'll jump on a bus later, visit his folks. He thought he might've been offered a double, double-time-and-a-half with the holiday, but with the place so quiet and everyone scrounging, the chances seem pretty slim. Friends in town invited him over, but they've got kids, and drink less. The day itself doesn't do much for him, not anymore, not for years. Each time round though he gives some thought to what was shoved down his throat before he had any arguments against the dogma. Back there deep in the fat of the head, the kind of diet you'd have to do to budge that shit, to get really clear of it. Gives some thought to Christ returned, but a Christ returned after God is dead. An orphan Christ, shuttled through foster homes. Christ with a depersonalization disorder. Christ with amnesia. Christ on glue. And what about Christ returned as a woman, daughter of God, there on the bed.

With the tossing and turning, her pyjama bottoms have worked down just below her hips, a finger-width of hair emerging up past the elastic band. Above that, dipping, the hollow of her gut, and on to where the skin swims up to the rib-cage ridge, then the p.j. top. The whole a kind of delicate crater, bright-moon-white against the cloth. Will she ask for the sponge, or must it be offered? And where, most humanely, to place the spear . . .

The nurse doing rounds comes around the corner and Rudy snaps clear and sees that what he can see can be seen from the hallway too, and when the nurse approaches his chair he tells her Carole's covers need adjustment, he didn't want to accidentally wake her, her finding him moving sheets across her body. The nurse understands and covers her up . . . Rudy prepared to protest his innocence . . . if need be . . . protest his guilt. The nurse signs off the round and relieves him.

Rudy stares at the space for his hour entry in the chart but nothing will come. Describe her sleep. Describe her breathing. Nothing will come. Describe her wounds.

"Wanna coffee?"

Rudy shakes his head.

"Eh?" Paul's back is turned.

"No."

"So where the hell's Jack? I wanna go home."

Rudy turns and shrugs as Paul shuffles back from the coffeepot.

"Y'seen that Kelly broad around recently?"

Rudy grunts no.

"Time she was in. 'Less she offed herself. That'd be a drag."

Rudy stretches.

"You know who I mean."

Rudy nods.

"Guess it's the meds, right . . . make her tits swell like that. Man, time before last, right, last time I was working days, but the time before that I was nights for a week. Man, she was frisky. Fuck like a mink . . . "

It starts to roll over Rudy like a wave.

"Head for a coffee . . . you never heard? Not like you had to come on to her or something. One night I'm sitting continuous, two a.m., she calls me in her room, she's by the closet, out of sight. Says she needs some help, one of the buttons on her shirt is stuck, all the others are undone, right, she's trying to change, she wants me to undo the last one, and I don't know, I figure if the meds have messed up her dexterity . . . so while I'm doing it — it *was* stuck, right? — no time at all she's got her hands down my pants and I'm hard as a rock and she climbs right on. Man, it's the fastest fuck I ever had, halfa me was shitting bricks 'case someone should come along, the other half was doing what comes naturally. Afterwards all she wanted was a cigarette. I thought wow and I'm the one bein' paid."

Jack, the night-shift supervisor, enters the station and gets himself a coffee. "What's the excitement?" he says routinely.

"So, Jack, I missed my break, right? Mind if I head home instead of pay?"

"No. Go ahead. We'll survive without you. Eh, Rudy?"

Rudy nods.

Paul dumps his coffee, grabs his coat, and slips Rudy a conspiring smirk.

"Merry Christmas."

"Merry Christmas."

Rudy, mute, turns back to the chart.

As the day staff start drifting in, Rudy wanders the last round. All the patients but one are sleeping, Carole having persuaded the nurse to let her into the lounge at seven. Rudy completes the row of S's but for her, gets his keys out and heads to the door. His path is blocked by Carole, smiling, her denture-plate in but with the teeth missing. She winks and says, "Hey, get me a Coke? from the machine?" and hands him several hot moist quarters. The nurse nods approval and Rudy goes out. The machine is out of Coke so he gets her a Pepsi, aware that this could initiate fireworks, goes back and slips it through the unit door.

"I wanted a Coke," he hears her voice.

"They run out of Coke." Then there's a silence. He passes the quarters back through the door. "They wouldn't take your money," he adds.

He's walking away. He hears, "Hey." He turns and sees her head sticking out, her body blocked by the nurse's arm.

"Hope Santa was good," she says. "Merry Christmas."
"Merry Christmas," Rudy says back.

He stands on the street in the freezing dawn, the temperature dropping an anchor over night, everywhere branches breaking from the weight of ice, everything crystal, the whole creaking street like bones in the wind, yet unburied. A polar wind pours over him — through him — and he looks into the blue shot through with wisps of white, bones so light they seem to float.

This lasts a moment, barely that. The chill takes hold, he shivers, then sees, some ten blocks down, the approaching streetcar.

Thinks of beer, numerous beers, waiting, cold, in the fridge at home. How many beers it will take to sleep, how many beers to float on that sea.

TOWARDS DEIRDRE'S

The first time I saw it, looked at that lake, I said notice the water: acidified. Clarity of water like that one does not get as a rule in a healthy lake — barring alpine, glacier-fed. Too clear by half. Take it as given. Dead before the mortgage is paid. Deirdre didn't either hear me or listen. I think it's pretty, was Marge's comment. Deirdre, down the slope a bit, was looking at the trees, trying (one assumes) to imagine what they'd look like with leaves on. A number stood between us and the lake. The structure was sound, the price within reason. The question had arisen as to whether or not the view would be jeopardized by full foliage. Late November it was hard to say. Most of the time would be spent there in summer, and little sense a good view in winter only come summer to have it marred by leaves. Prettiness isn't the issue, I said. Marge took a deep breath. Screams are not unheard of. Instead she gave a fatuous smile and said no one here decided the issue. Which was true, in strictest terms. I said, be that as it may.

Deirdre, regardless, purchased the property. Cash down. Marge was thrown. She asked me later where I thought she got the cash from. Beats me, I said. It wasn't our business. Marge maintained it was; as family, one likes to know how one's sibling is doing. Meaning hers. I shrugged. I said, perhaps she got an advance from the publisher. Marge said nothing, she looked me over.

Deirdre didn't make it down for Christmas. She stayed on the lake in her bungalow, working on her book on God. Marge hadn't pushed it. The book's a critique. Marge likes her Christmas with some of the ritual. Past years they'd managed to agree on a tree, but Deirdre the last time had made a joke about the angel impaled on top. Boxing Day I'd inadvertently stepped back on the manger scene, it broke, there were parts in need of repair I'd left spread out on the coffee table. Deirdre had used the cradle for an ashtray. Marge got upset, it was a real misunderstanding. Deirdre and I both said we were sorry, but Marge had her doubts, she subscribes to Freud. Think we should get her down, she'd asked me, this time? but it wasn't a question. Maybe leave it up to her, she continued, let her know she's welcome, so long as she's willing to show some respect. But Deirdre didn't come, and Marge then felt guilty. Christmas was quiet, but nothing went wrong.

Winter proceeded. It was almost spring before the issue of Deirdre's came up again. A woman in Marge's Amnesty group had buried a sister the week before, they hadn't said goodbye, it was all the woman could do to drag herself out to the meeting. The sisters had not talked in eight years. This is how it starts, said Marge, reminding me I had some time coming. I told her the car would need to be looked at. Precautionary-wise. She did not flinch. I said it could add up to a bundle. You don't want to go, she said. It's not that, I said, it's a five-hour drive, it's out in the middle of nowhere is all. Suit yourself, I'm going, she said.

The car had been if nothing else reliable. Bought it thinking we might have kids. The warranty ran out a few years ago, but nothing happened, suddenly, of note. Marge feels for the world, I think that's the trouble. She wants — or rather cannot grasp why the world doesn't operate the way she thinks it should. I dropped by Émile's. His accent sometimes, whether exacerbated by the moustache, a sprawling affair — or not, I've been tempted — or was, at first — to wonder if it wasn't — how should I say — a touch *put on*? Have to get his quotations in writing. I voiced some concerns re brake caliper lockup, misfiring pistons, the hole in the floorboard. He watches one speak, he pays full attention, he watches the mouth as one's words come out, as though he were deaf, though I know he's not, his face at best impassive, his own mouth concealed by that daunting barricade of hair. Not that it interferes with his work. It's just not so common, growth to that degree. He did what he could, time being a factor, the floor he said would have to wait — for welding — in the meantime throw a pillow down. I took it as jargon. *Pillow*? I said. An old one, he qualified. Engine's fine. Exhaust system ditto.

On the way back I stopped in at the liquor store. Marge was home packing. I thought about the pillow. I picked up some wine, something, a gesture. I picked up some Scotch for myself and, so as not to forget, tucked it under the seat. I couldn't recollect a store near Deirdre's. Her lips are red, vibrantly so. She doesn't wear lipstick, it's pigmentary. She only drinks red, which makes it easy — thinking of her lips, what it is that she drinks. Marge drinks white, her lips you hardly notice. Not that one has to, that lips should draw notice.

I came in the door and Marge was standing with her coat on looking out the window by the sink. Almost for a moment I didn't recognize her. She was far away, someone else. She turned and fixed on the liquor store bag. I thought we might bring some wine, I said, took out the bottle and placed it on the table. I'd made a mistake, the wine was white. Oh, she said, for me, that's sweet. Her one eye, just the one, was wet. We should pick some up for Deirdre, she said, she only drinks red. I nodded.

It was late afternoon before we got going but the traffic wasn't bad. Marge was driving. The last we heard from the doctor he said he wasn't sure — more tests were needed — but suspected her eggs were allergic to my sperm. I looked out the window at the trees, the evergreens darkly dominant over the hills. Here and there a stand of birch, gnarled though and dying off, granite outcrops, places the Shield had to be blasted to put through the road. Lovers' graffiti. Other inanities.

Marge was having no luck with stations. She likes human interest, she was searching for a phone-in. The phone-ins, I said, are predominantly morning. She was not deterred. I stared out ahead. The road was better than one might expect. A fellow I know, an authority on pavement, said these in particular required constant maintenance, the freezing and thawing tore them apart. You want to talk taxes, he liked to say, add up repairs to roads to bloody nowhere. Bias was apparent, yet he had a point. Marge's minister suggested prayer, that it cannot hurt — there too a bias. I tried once actually — this was some time ago — just for interest, but it didn't feel right. Not saying I'd rule it out entirely — *one man's meat . . .* — but I'd exercise caution.

Deirdre would have us believe she's happy. Angry too, but that's another item. Marge says she hasn't woken up, that life is not one entire vacation, spending half the year on the lake, the other half pushing one's luck in Mexico. She owns the bungalow, has a car, but no steady job, no boyfriend we know of. Marge is concerned Deirdre's wasting her life, that rain has yet to locate her parade. But when it does . . . I told her some parades carry on in spite of rain. She's not your sister, Marge has me know. Marge is older, almost three years.

What happens when she's older, says Marge, when Deirdre is older, when she's lost her looks. Implicit the question of income.

I was having problems with a crossword. I asked her was she tired. She shook her head. Dusk had obliterated much of the landscape. I needed a four-letter word for *peculiar* beginning with a *c*. Marge stopped for Certs, Ritz crackers and coffee. I declined the latter, I was feeling some acidity. Tums, I mentioned as she got out, but apparently she did not hear me. Gas was exorbitant, we still had half a tank, we knew of a cheaper place near Deirdre's. I leaned against the car while Marge used the toilet. I've always enjoyed that, stopped at stations en route, leaning against one's vehicle, before recommencing with the journey in question. The wind had come up and clouds were building. The temperature hung a bit below zero. Another two hours, said Marge as we got back in. That's hoping, I said. Re the conditions. She didn't like my tone.

We pulled out and soon enough a light snow was falling. Can you check the map, she said, whereabouts we turn. I took it out and looked. Maps I find deceptive. We have several options, we could stay on this, or take the next turn-off, it seems, I said. Folding the map I returned it to the dashboard. You said several, that's two, said Marge. The problem here — which we'd dealt with before — is that I use *several* interchangeably with *two*. I don't restrict it to *two*, but I use it. Marge maintains that this is erroneous, that several is *more than two but not many*. The dictionary leans her way. I don't protest. Two then, all right? I said. Marge said, that's different. Two then, this or the next, I repeated. Perhaps with an edge. No sooner said than the first rose up rapidly in our lights. Marge didn't slow. The sign as we passed it I noticed was riddled with bulletholes, the 7 all but gone. A ways back we'd passed a sign for a moose crossing. The moose had been intact. I wondered why the moose and why not the 7. The moose would seem more logical fare. But of course the moose was not a moose, a symbol rather, an emblem of a moose. The number 7 was essentially that. A man could go home and say, I shot a 7. Not so the moose. Whether that was why.

Metal fatigue leapt to mind. The expression. At first I thought *mental* fatigue, but quickly concluded that was not it. Mental fatigue is a common state, but the thought that *metal* at any given moment is perhaps approaching some critical threshold, beyond which loomed — what, if not collapse? We were in a car, a thing made of metal.

Slip me a Ritz, I heard Marge say. A mutter briefly cresting the defrost. I reached down to get them and noticed the draft, a slight but steady stream at my foot. I repositioned the pillow and found it damp, the underside stiffening. I opened the box. Just the one? I asked. Several, said Marge, and found this amusing. She being the driver I let her have her joke.

The snow continued as is its wont. Marge let up on the gas a bit, but grudgingly — given our schedule. I kept my eyes peeled for the second turn-off, but drifting and gusts made it difficult. Remember the camera? Marge said through crackers. Yes, I said, though in fact I couldn't. I knew I'd thought about bringing it. Where? she asked. In the trunk, I suggested. It's safe there? she followed. It's locked, I said. I mean the cold, Marge said with some impatience, won't the film crack or something if it gets too cold? Good, I informed her, to twenty below. It seemed plausible enough, it put her mind at rest.

Marge's bringing up the camera surprised me. Not since Deirdre's last birthday had we used it. Marge was taking a course at the time, it was partly her fault, she composed the picture. Deirdre sitting peering up at the camera, her blouse partially open — summer, with the heat. Marge feels — and makes it no secret — that bangs are wrong for a woman Deirdre's age, bangs that spill down over the eyes, that obscure the vision and shadow the face. Don't they drive you crazy, she says, when what she means is they make her look cheap. I'm in profile. Deirdre's wearing these interesting beads she'd come upon in Mexico, I'd only then noticed them, and that was why. Marge — as she often does — cut off my head, but cut it high enough up on the forehead it's plain as day where my glance is directed. The problem was the beads had slipped behind the blouse. From the camera's vantage point they are not apparent. I thought at first of putting it aside, I'd had them developed, I had first access, but Marge knew the shots, to the F-stop and shutter speed, the negatives existed, it would take an Act of God. The shot in fact had an interesting quality, given the exposure, the partially severed head. Had we been strangers she'd have probably been quite happy. As it was she dropped the course.

An unmarked exit appeared on the left. Marge slowed. I thought it ought to be marked, if an exit of significance, there ought to be some suggestion, sign. She brought the car to a full stop. The snow lay deep and undisturbed. Perhaps we should verify our bearings, I said. Where else could we be? she threw back, then made the turn. Fine in theory. I took up the crossword. You know your way from here, I said. Don't sulk, she said. I'm not sulking, I told her. Her glance remained a challenge. All right, I said: a nine-letter word for *messy situation* beginning with a *p*. The *p* was conjecture, it might have been a *p*. A *p* was as likely as anything. Whether she gave it thought or not, we drove on, into the white.

How's the pillow? her voice came out of nowhere. I looked across and she met my look. I tried to nudge it, but my foot would not respond. I reached down and bent the foot this way and that, but the rubber of the overshoe resisted massage. I worked down the zipper, got an index finger in, squeezed it under the tongue of the loafer . . .

Without warning I'm catapulted forward. Head meets dashboard, glove compartment opens, out fall pencils, coupons, tire-pressure gauges, small change, maintenance guides. I feel my stomach climbing my throat, I wrench my head and fix on Marge. She's pumping the brake, clenching the wheel, preoccupied — as it were — with a skid. She steers correctly into it, the brakes do not lock, inertia diminishes, she eases back slightly in her seat, the blur out the window resolving to snowflakes slanting past in gentle descent. I raise my head above the dash, look out and see not thirty feet away, standing in the middle of the road, a horse.

Sorry, says Marge, it just appeared. She honks but the horse in no way responds. It's at a diagonal, facing away. North-north-east, ass facing us. I look around and see we're intact and am about to commend her on her driving. That horse, she says, has no business being there. She adds she thinks I should shoo it away. I let this sink in. Flurries. No witnesses. Well, I say, and if it disobeys? All I meant was I couldn't see why a horse in the middle of a country road would pay any heed to directions from strangers. Marge sighed. It could've got ugly.

I open the door and climb out. We're closer to the shoulder than I'd realized. My sleeping foot meets the ground — or so I guess — I stumble but recover. My next step takes me to the hips in snow. Perhaps the air, the oddity . . . I think to make an angel — but then see the horse. It's where it was, it has not moved. I wade a few yards till I'm back out on asphalt. The high beams throw me huge against the night. Ego's not at issue here, my shadow's inconvenient, obscuring within it the problematic horse. I wave back to Marge and she dims the lights. I move toward it, free of bias. A luminous grey, large, of the work type. Feces down one leg — it's funny — the feces, the *shit*, the shit actually somehow broke the ice, made things less formal. Its body covered — lacquered — in sweat, gleaming, and steam ascending, curling up and over the impressive haunches, larger than one tends to expect, to think horses get, that large, to that dimension. The idea, then, was to try not to spook it.

There came the point the crossing of which placed one further from the car than the horse. Spatially. It seemed tame. Comfortably oriented, at its ease, neither agitated nor inclined to move. I got as close as seemed feasible, then made the standard shooing motion. The word may or may not have crossed my lips — *shoo* — a sequence of two, then a pause, repeated, and so on — I don't remember. I do remember the sudden — the twisting of muscles in the neck — the turning of its head.

A whiteout, swift and absolute, descended on our portion of the road. I dropped to the ground and covered my face. Time slid, replaced by an image: a little glass ball filled with water and plastic flakes, the globe inverted then turned right-side up, the flakes gradually settling back through the fluid. Often it's a cottage scene in the woods, as was this, and a figure — Deirdre. Her Japanese robe open at the throat, a descending V past collarbone, sternum, almost solar plexus, before the V concludes in the dark overhang thrown by the arcs of the bosom. She's bending over, gathering flowers, bright red inexplicable blooms (red of a wavelength that leaps at the eye, hence its utilization in stop signs) rising up, disrupting the white. Type of flower tough to gauge, the snow itself more like fog, or down, impeding her little as she wades. She reaches for a flower, the robe — though sashed —

straining to contain the renegade chest, the wedge clearly widening, warping the otherwise rigid line of the two converging planes, the flesh therewithin a sea of turmoil, symmetric contours, parabolic interstices — then, the flower picked, she stands.

Taking a fist, the one free of flowers, she knuckles in at a muscle knot. Lumbodorsal, common enough. One breast juts out free of the robe, and on the lower inner slope, like a dark moon rising, a tiny mole. What precisely it was about the mole, its seeming centricity — *fixedness* — around which all else seemed to move . . .

Deirdre folds the breast back in, raises her face, and looks across. Beneath the bangs the eyes do not flicker. She tightens the sash. One hopes for a smile. But the mouth stays closed, offers nothing but shade for two rows of teeth and a tongue. She puts the flowers in a cracked pot, takes up the axe and begins to split wood.

Whatever it was was warm and moved across my face and hands like a breath. Sound returned, the honk of the horn. I pried the loosened ice from my lids. The road, as far as one could see, lay quiet and empty, but for us. Those headlights — halos — Marge at the wheel. I crawled, I don't know why I crawled, but I crawled the distance back to the car, opened the passenger side and climbed in. Marge was hunched toward the dashboard, prowling the dial for intelligible noise. I asked her had she seen the horse go. She hadn't, it was dark, when she'd turned on the lights she'd seen me curled up, but that was all. I wanted to talk some more about the horse but Marge would not respond to my leads. It was just a horse, she finally said. On the third passage down the dial distinctive notes broke from the buzz. She gave me a look, but left it on station. Bizet's *Carmen*, Neville Marriner conducting. Opera drives her up the wall. After a while, with no voices coming, she seemed relieved, though on her guard. Symphonic, I said, there won't be any voices. What she would have preferred was talk, the chatter and yap of total strangers alive at this moment somewhere in the world. We're of different ilks. Still, it was a gesture.

Down the road a little ways she turned and said to me, something the matter? I'd say there was, though in point of fact I didn't, I saw no sense in making a scene. My foot was stiff, I felt she'd been distant, I wanted to be at home with a book. One could not say the weather got worse but it did not improve, the snow continued, the road — with no other vehicles on it — became less and less distinct as a road. The music, somewhere between two lakes, slipped from the dial and even Marge seemed to sense its desertion. We crept on. I can't say how long I was aware of the little gold glow in the darkest corner of the instrument panel before I acknowledged it. Marge too perhaps saw no purpose. The needle had hovered at "E" for some time. The appearance of the fuel-pump symbol was at least one more light in the surrounding dark. All one had to do was squint and it could as easily be that of a candle.

Marge took her foot off the pedal and let us coast to a stop, tried the radio again but found only crackle interspersed with hiss. Brief snatches of utter silence. *Dead air*, as they say in the trade. Well? she said, and put the car in Park. He too serves, I said, who sits and waits. She didn't find this funny and told me, which was fine, I had other reasons, among them a seeking of perspective. I took the Scotch from beneath the seat. Actually the concept of serving repels me, I don't even like it in restaurants. I took a sip. Marge looked hurt. I offered her some but she turned away. We're not going anywhere immediately, I said. And if, she responded, someone were to find us, me at the wheel, Scotch on my breath? I didn't pursue it. I had another sip. Besides, she added, it does the opposite, *lowers* body temperature, it does not *raise* it, it's only an illusion, dangerous at that. Thanks, I said, and drank.

Twenty-odd minutes of idling did the gas. The engine coughed, shuddered, then quit. Shortly thereafter the vent-air went cool. I took the keys, got out and stood in the snow. Stood in a manner. Lacking sensation below the shin, I kept the knee rigid and used the leg as, normally, one might a crutch. The sky was now clear and moonless, the air seemed — maybe in my numbness — mild. It crossed my mind to hurl the keys away, as far as I could, into the trees. It made no sense. Thus the temptation.

Sitting on the bumper, giving this some thought, I noticed the cold begin to eat through my trousers. A fire, I thought. A fire might be nice. I opened the trunk, took out some blankets and threw them into the front seat. Marge was staring out ahead, at what I don't know, there wasn't much to see. I went back, took out the spare, a litre of all-season motor oil, laid the tire on the road, poured the oil across the tire. I hadn't a match. The panel lighter. I went back, opened the driver's door, reached past Marge and pushed in the button. What are you doing? she managed vaguely. Setting the spare on fire, I said. A ripple of quandary creased her brow. Tell me when it pops, I said. As I closed the door I noticed the Scotch open in her lap, crumbs of Ritz crackers, the foil from the Certs.

Above, the stars were confounding as ever. Seeming to signal, seeming to mean, and yet not offering anything concrete. There comes a point one considers the planet, one's placement here, the pros and cons. There's something a touch precarious, to my mind, something a little too hit-and-miss. I had no Carborundum in the car, no molten lava, no kite and storm. I had a wife ensconced at the wheel, some scotch, a crossword, a registered vehicle. A map which may as well have been for Mars. I have little patience with the noble savage theory. I don't think karma is a ludicrous notion, but I would not bet my bottom dollar on it. I agree with separating church and state, can accept that dinosaurs were likely wiped out by climatic change due to dust thrown up by one (albeit large) meteor, that we're born if not in sin at least flawed. I like the use of *several*, and of *one*, I find them civilized and calming. All that said, no gods intervened. I knocked on the window and found Marge asleep, covered her with blankets, the lighter hadn't popped, I checked and found it not even warm. *Kyrie eleison*, so they say. Sleep overtook me in the passenger seat, poised beside Marge, though not quite so bundled.

One only knows one has slept — and not died — by waking, which we did come dawn. A Christmas-tree farmer out plowing his road (the one on which we'd ended up) rapped on the window, I stirred, as did Marge. The morning was bright and clear as an insult, with spring surely on the breeze. He siphoned some gas from his tank to ours, gave us a jump, returned the soiled spare without comment to the trunk, then led us back to a gas station we'd inexplicably passed in the night. They had a phone which Marge went and used. I turned on the radio, reception was excellent, the bantering voices giddy almost, as though the aggressive cloying good nature was adequate anchor. I shook my head. It was a phone-in show. I thought to go and give them a ring, once Marge was finished, subject them to an earful, and might have if my feet had moved. The farmer stuck his head in the window. I sensed he'd found my stupor odd. You okay? he said with some concern. Okay, I said, is one tall order.

I don't know, to say *surprised*, given the contingencies, is asking a bit. The hole in the floorboard, my poor circulation, the blizzard, the horse, the unzipped zipper . . . leave alone Deirdre and her book on God. Still, to wake — *wake* is a fine word — to wake and find they've severed your toes. I looked at the foot. It was bandaged quite neatly, it looked like a present at the end of the bed. Nothing short of tracing the leg down the covers supported the theory it was mine. The doctor came in and stood to one side. Cut off the actual toes, I said. That or the actual leg, he responded. In his hand a sheet of paper on which I could make out my scribbled consent. Marge's too. I had no recollection. How many? I asked. Several, he answered. Perhaps I flinched. Three, if I'm not mistaken, he added. Portion of the fourth, but the big toe's intact. The big toe . . . , I started but lost my train. Intact, he said, yes. Would there, I ventured, be some residual . . . *effect* . . . ? He finished, to the gait? — none to speak of, the big toe the bastion of the terminal support. He made no bones, I could thank my lucky stars, infection would have spread up the leg, poisoned the bloodstream, one could gather the rest. Immediate? I queried. Rapid, he said, and his eyebrows rose in emphasis. A moment later they began the return to their pre-emphatic position on his face. I wanted to laugh but managed to restrain myself. I had no proof he would readily join in. To laugh alone invites certain risks. Consequences. I hadn't the strength.

Beyond the toes we had little in common. He stood there, one hand supporting the chin, staring at the bandaged foot, as though in some sort of grim anticipation. It wasn't a terribly awkward silence, I was too dazed and he too absorbed. Marge came in, buoyant, with flowers. She stood at first at the end of the bed. From where the doctor stood I suppose the flowers could seem to have sprouted from the foot. I watched him give a little shudder, mutter some pleasantry, then make his way out.

I'm not and never was much one for flowers, cut that is, removed from soil. Stuck in a vase, withering with every glance a little more. Gets so one avoids looking over, so as not to be complicit, not escalate the process. Marge of course asked me how I liked them. I was honest. She took it in stride. She said she was happy to see me myself. We chatted a bit. She mentioned there had been a moment in the car when she almost gave up, got out and walked away in the white. The unlit white. I thought, hmmmm. She turned she said and saw me asleep, listened to my snore, there was something in the snore. She'd thought she was going mad she said, drawn to that snore, held in its grip. *Mad* — and the word hung from her lip, dangled in the chill arid air of that room, then trembled, dropped like a petal, spiralled down and broke apart on her blouse. She continued to speak. I found myself fixed on a gap between buttons through which flesh could be glimpsed. Suddenly it dawned on me — the breast had been hers. Marge's, the mole on the left inner slope. There wasn't any question. As for the head . . .

Something the matter? came Marge's voice, and I looked up, noting the absence of tone usually attendant on that phrase. A cautious smile, a curious smile. I shook my head. Save the toes, I said. Her smile withered, and froze on her face. Topple a gargoyle. It took me a moment. *Save* as in *except*, I said. Oh, said Marge, and her buoyancy returned. You're fine? I asked. She nodded, sighed, and looked about the room. Her glance came to rest on a book of crosswords a nurse, having heard of my interest, left. *P*, said Marge, it wasn't a *p* . . . your word, what it started with . . . the word was *imbroglio*. I let this sink in. The night in the car. I didn't much care and shrugged in accordance. Usually a shrug of mine would end a conversation. Marge won't abide them, not as a rule. This time however she looked across, considered me a moment, then patted my arm, as though the shrug had never occurred. This felt odd. I thought, perhaps she missed it. Once, with a blind man, I'd found myself having to take my shrugs, wrestle and warp and grind them into words, often poorly. That was translation though, not repetition. Shrugs are part of spontaneous being. It's like being asked to repeat one's laugh. Gradually I realised she had no such intention, the shrug — for all its careful ambivalence — was lost to time, would not come again. It struck me it might be a ploy on her part, henceforth to fully ignore my shrugs, forcing me to accept her statements or challenge them in the full light of dialogue.

Out of the blue she patted me again. I almost recoiled it was so unexpected. Not as though she were patting a cat or a dog or a cushion on which someone should sit. It was genuine. Not, of course, meaning that with dogs or cats the pats are less genuine. Just that with animals the means are restricted by which to convey rapport, connection, sympathy, like-mindedness. With me she could've easily used words, but didn't, she made a point of taking off her glove, of using her hand, her skin against mine. Her skin seemed unusually soft. I mentioned this. She seemed pleased. Cream she said that Deirdre sent, had arrived that day along with Deirdre's best. I nodded. Nice, no? she added re the cream. Ending affirmatives with their negation, it's a quirk of hers, I don't know where she gets it. I smiled nonetheless. Yes, I said, it's nice. She placed her hand back on my arm.

I thought about the floorboard, the hole in the floorboard, perhaps to mention to make an appointment with Emile, his garage, to have it fixed. Even Marge trusts Emile, she says it's the moustache, grown with such abandon, much like the one she claims her grandfather had. The rest of the face clean as a whistle. It had crossed my mind on occasion in the past, but the thing demands patience, a fair density of follicles, upkeep, and caution with various foods. I'd last attempted a moustache in college, but it had not survived the week home at Christmas. Sheared, for the most part, daily since, it held completely unmeasured potential. I looked at Marge. She was holding my hand, turning it this way and that between her own. My hands are quite average. It was not that. I watched her. I could not look away.

THE SITUATION WHAT IT DOES
TO HIM PERSONALLY

Trout season opened today. Crept up on him. Never before. Because of the dream, the nurse going on, if she hadn't made the deal she did about a dream where nothing happened, or things did but not with people, there wasn't anybody, he killed nobody, in the dream he was just there, standing there at the top of the world, watching.

Each his own. What it was with her. Eyelids flapping like wounded ducks. And him there thinking with a dream so empty she'd let it pass, she wouldn't push, she'd leave him alone, they all would.

Parking lot in winter, how it seemed most. Shopping mall without the mall. Curved, flat, white. Instead of lines on where to park were knobs galore, with wires attached, ankle-height, like tripwires. Trapdoors opening here and there with stuff coming out — appliances. Not just toasters, all sorts of things. When he tries to visualize it he cannot be sure there's even a toaster. Air feels hollow. No point breathing. Don't need to move. You get that feeling. Just this stuff coming out of the ground, slow motion, no end in sight.

She asked him where he thought it was.

"The place things come from," Larry said.

He's eating peas. What they call peas. They're green and circular, most of them. She asked if there wasn't some kind of animal, bird or fish or various creature. He figured odds were that down those holes were probably rats or mice like they had in the warehouse, but seeing how he hadn't actually seen one, he could not say for absolute sure. The peas taste like nothing, even less than the fish, which he cannot eat even though he is hungry. He tried the fish but it broke apart on his tongue into particles tasting like even less than before, if that's possible. Anything's possible here in this place. There's one guy hauling a hanger on wheels, a bag of sugar-water on the hanger, a tube running down from the bag to his arm where it disappears beneath a bandage. The fish smells like lemon but tastes like nothing. The peas which are not circular are mush. In the confusion. Moss paste. Could be worse. He could be the guy getting filled up with water. Swimming inside. Thing is, from outside the guy looks dry. Dry as a bone. Which maybe is the problem.

Larry does not deny his mental state. But what he did he *knows* was wrong, and a thing a normal person could have done, someone with a temper or a chip on the shoulder or a whole bag of stresses, to do what he did. You do not have to be mad is his point. To do what he did. He could've been normal.

There was a dream with living things in it, but that was in Detention, the night before transfer. With Daryl Hannah, the mermaid from *Splash*. She wasn't a mermaid, she was just a person, she had all her clothes on, he kicked himself later thinking if it was his dream why'd she have to keep her clothes on? In the dream they were just like friends, they hadn't met in years but had necked once in high school. They go into a bar and talk a while, it's like real life till they go outside. He finds out someone's stolen his bike, with all his paper route papers in the carrier. It hits him he hasn't finished his deliveries. It's late afternoon. It's an early morning route. She tells him it's okay and kisses his cheek. She says she'll drop by later.

When he wakes up he's in this great mood, and it lasts the better part of the day. Transfer cross-town to Forensic, admission, orientation, a reheated lunch of corned beef and sauerkraut, through Dave with the nose scanning the radio dial at top volume every ten seconds, through even the guy with the scabs — Gavin — bugging him three times for cigarettes. It lasts until when they head down for volleyball, the ones allowed, and he watches them go. The door closes in front of him and through the wire-reinforced glass he sees the elevator doors open and the unit guys get on and they move to one side because on the other, the side by the buttons, there's a doctor in a lab coat and someone — a secretary? — blond and slim and tall and could pass, if you squinted, for Daryl Hannah. It hits him then and there like a brick, when the doors close, when he's left behind, it hits him that he does not know Daryl Hannah. There's no two ways around it. No way at all.

The dark cloud fact of not knowing Daryl Hannah hung over him half the week. Found her picture on the cover of *People,* second night in, a beat-up copy that'd done the rounds, and he stared at it on and off for two days. He'd feel the vein in his temple squirming like a worm trapped between the skull and skin, trying to get out, but no one came in while this was happening, he'd stare at the glare coming off her sunglasses, wondering why she'd betray him like that, he never did anything to her he knows of, then someone called down *supper* and he found himself working through peas and fish he could not taste.

After supper, returning to his room, he wonders if it really was her in the dream or someone who only looked like her. No one in the dream actually said it was her, he didn't call her that, he knows he didn't, he can't see calling a woman *Daryl.* He sits on his bed and looks at the picture. His anger, strangely enough, is gone. She looks like anyone famous, unreal.

Ed comes into the room sometime then and puts a paper plate down near Larry, on it a piece of cherry pie. He says, "I thought you might want your pie. It's Larry, right?"

Larry looks up and Ed, he sees, is the guy they put in the far corner bed in the three-bed room the night before when Larry, face-down, pretended to sleep, a blanket across him so no passing creep would see it as an invitation. Ed was the guy humming "King of the Road," till they tried to take his belt, a nurse did, and never before'd Larry heard someone go to such lengths to prove to a person — in this case the nurse — the need for a thing. For Ed, it was a Peterbilt buckle, he gave up the belt, he fully saw the reasoning, but held that the buckle posed no threat, had no sharp edges, couldn't be swallowed, had just a blunt hook to hold the belt holes, he pressed and pressed till the nurse relented, so long as he was fully aware that possessions lost or stolen were not the responsibility of the nursing staff. The buckle now dangles gleaming from the pocket buttonhole of Ed's denim jacket. His face is a doormat reading "Welcome." He holds out a handful of scarred and grease-dark fingers, a palm of knit muscle off a wrist like a pipe.

"Ed," says Ed. "I'm bunked out over there." And a slight toss of the head wrenches free a coil of oiled greying hair from the mass on top, and it dangles down. He and Larry watch it a moment. "Drive me goddam cross-eyed," he says, then rakes it back with his left hand, the right remaining extended.

It's way past what Larry would think someone would hazard, to hold out your hand that long to a stranger. Larry finally reaches out his, they shake, it's firm but not a competition. "Penny ante in the lounge later, if you're game," Ed adds, on release. Larry does not commit himself. Ed doesn't push it, he seems to know that much, he nods, turns and walks out, leaving Larry to his cherry pie, magazine, ruminations.

Does playing cards show a lack of remorse? Is skill at poker a sanity gauge? For the first time Larry wonders what the others have done. Ed. Gavin. The kid he saw wielding her chest like a trophy, or maybe a curse.

At nine p.m., with meds being dispensed, Larry wagers the toilet might be quiet. He can't ever shit with others nearby, sphincter locks, nothing will move. But going in he hears someone in one of the stalls, but only one. He goes to the sink and washes his face, washes his hands, looks in the mirror, the lights above making caves of his eyes, his brow blazing white, cheekbones too, the broken bridge of nose, the skull visible right through the hair — in fact, everywhere there isn't a hole — eye, mouth, nostril — leaking dark. Looks like a ghost of himself he's looking at, never seen or imagined a sicker-looking ghost than this, maybe that's normal, that the scariest ghost would be your own. He stops the tap and listens. Grunts — groaning, suction, breath, and grunts. He then hears a slight gasp for air, a slosh, a muffled crush of flesh. He crouches down and looks beneath the stall-boards, sees the guy's feet, heels off the tiles, tensed, pants at the ankles like he's giving birth. Then a thin hand drifts down, palm to the tile, the opposite direction. Painted nails, impossible they're, the angle, the tiny wrists, knuckles flexing. The feet rock in spasm, a wave of flowered skirt floats down and curtains the shoes. Larry, his face inches from the floor, hauls in a breath and with it a wave of mingled fumes — tile antiseptic, citrus soap, piss, sweat, pine cones, and cum. The cum comes last to his registration, tangled up, his & hers. He sees the woman's feet meet the floor, he's up in a flash to the sink, his head submerged in white, the faucet blasting, but blood is slow getting up to his head and his hands have to latch, lock on to the sides of the sink which then can fly wherever, hands a bridge between it and the wrists which lead to the arms the shoulders the neck his head where there is this void, sure, for a minute, but the minute will pass. Like it always does.

The comets subside. Their dimming trails slip to patterns of the concrete world — a square sink, metallic wall cylinder with squirt-pump valve and a quart of pink soap, a wall, the rim of a rapidly defogging mirror, toothpaste constellations, an oval and lame excuse for a face — Larry's — trying to stay within the lines.

There's a laugh, or less. Deep, but not a man's. He turns and sees a woman beside him, next sink over, touching up her make-up. A flowered dress, hair of soft snakes, face calm plain and featureless until she turns and opens her mouth. "You're new," she says, and her tongue is a drowsy stretching creature on a bone-white ledge.

Larry swallows, then clears his throat, as though there were anything but fear left in it. Unsure where the blood will go next, he turns and makes for the door. If she opens her mouth again — but she doesn't. He turns to make sure, sees the back of her head as she bends to within inches of the mirror. Another few seconds, he knows, if he waits, the glass will go fluid and she'll pass right through. He grounds himself between door and jamb, awaiting whatever, the flowers to creep from the dress on vines, entwine his legs, or her to turn *without any face*, the room to spin, his heart explode . . .

All that comes is a hand to his arm from the hall, a nurse's aide. Larry crosses the hall, turns back, and watches the man prop the door with his foot. "Madelaine," he says, "we've been through all this." He holds the door as she filters past.

"I was freshening up. The women's was steamy. Ask him," and she nods to Larry. "I didn't do anything. Search me if you want." She continues off and down the hall, her wake a sinuous cloud of talcum, cinnamon, and cigarette. The flowers in her dress fairly wave.

"Maybe you should talk to your nurse," the aide tells Larry. "Just a thought."

Madelaine calls from down the hall, "Snack," and gradually the men make their way.

Four-to-one odds on rain overnight, up from two since the weather forecast. The couch boys ask if Larry wants in. Larry's neck cranks his face their way, but his mind does not follow. They write him off. His face swings back to an approximate fix on the TV eight feet up in a corner, pulsing alpha, pulsing omega. His nurse got pulled early in shift so the talk the aide suggested they have did not happen. Madelaine has drifted by since, but her looks were neutral, even warm. In the kangaroo pocket of his hooded sweatshirt Larry works the handle of his Shakespeare reel. Methodically, a variable tick, a clock he can control.

He thinks of a stream he knew as a kid, with dangerous stretches of rapid, eddy, and undertow, where a kid he knew drowned. One night afterward he lay in bed, dreamed of that water, went under, swam around. He saw fish, saw the drowned kid, who'd gone a bit metallic and talked in bubbles, weird riddle-messages for Larry to take back. In daylight, awake, he returned to the stream. He'd throw in his line and the fish would strike like mad, like they recognized him. He threw most back. Some days it was enough to sit, stare at the

water, think about below. He'd half-watch for the face of the
kid, silver, slipping through weed beds, lily pads, or just in
the shadow of a rotting log. He never saw it, but sometimes,
thinking he'd heard a word, he'd turn and see bubbles. The
word was never anything clear, a made-up word, what a kid
might invent. An underwater kid.

His line on the TV is blocked by Tania standing in front of
him, staring at the wall. She ended up beside him at snack,
gave him a capsule version of her life. The kid with the chest.
Not so much a kid as he thought, twenty, bone-thin, with
fried brains, pellucid skin, and cut-rate breast implants that
have started to drift. She's in for shoplifting, cosmetics and
glue. "So what's that, a shark or what?" she says. Her jaw jerks
out at a Doodle-Art poster on the wall beside him, a spec-
trum of wildlife with fish at the bottom, brightly coloured
with inconsistent concern for line or species or element. Larry
spots the creature in question, a yellow armoured tube with
purple fins.

"Sturgeon," he tells her, "or that's what it was."

"Huh."

"Bottom-feeder. Get pretty big."

"Ugly sucker."

"They're not that colour."

"Still."

"Yeah. 'S where they get caviar."

"No shit."

"Really."

"Man, who'd a thought."

She takes a seat and offers him a cigarette. He shakes his
head. It's the late-night news. They both sort of watch but he
finds himself thinking of that sturgeon in the Fraser, a hundred years old. Two guys got stopped on a routine booze
check, the cops pulling back their pickup's tarp, perhaps the

smell alerting them. Caught in possession of a century-old fish. Got a fish scientist to figure out the age. Strange part is he feels sorry for the fish. To make it over a hundred years, then get snagged by some jokers on a weekend. He wonders what the sturgeon was thinking, hauled into air after a century. Must've been strange — unless it just gave up, unless it just got tired of fighting the current.

"UFOs," he hears Tania say.

He sees it's an item on those circles, the ones in the wheat fields, the speculation.

"UFOs — right!" snorts one of the guys.

Gavin comes in and joins the couch.

"She says they're UFOs."

"What?"

"What caused those circles."

The item ends and Gavin looks across. "Only UFOs are the ones over there," and he nods to Tania's chest. The guys beside him follow in his gaze.

A nurse's aide appears in the doorway.

"Guess they're still a mystery to you, huh?" says Tania.

Gavin blushes and hates himself for it. "Should've got a brain put in while they were at it."

Larry feels Tania's nails sink into his wrist.

"Gavin," says the nurse's aide, and a nod suggests Gavin join him in the hall. Gavin furtively tugs out his shirt-tails, and saunters a wide arc out of Tania's reach.

The couch boys grudgingly drag their eyes away.

Tania's grip loosens on Larry's arm, she removes her hand, and he watches the fierce white impression fade with returning blood. The late-night movie is coming on, Cary Grant and Katharine Hepburn. She shifts in her seat and their shoulders touch. Larry freezes, not even sure what the wrong move is.

Larry is not asleep but is only made conscious of this by Ed's voice, low, insistent, snaking through the medicated air.

"Larry, you asleep?"

"Almost."

He'd been thinking of the first fish he caught — found, more like — a sucker from a pond on top of the Niagara escarpment. Rubs the scar he has to show. The sucker had thrown itself up on the rocks, bleeding from the gills, mouth. He got to it first, but only barely, Allan Bailey was right behind. The thing was huge, twenty pounds, and Allan said he'd seen it first. Larry disagreed and Allan went berserk. They were both about nine. Allan would calm down some years later, but at that time the smallest frustration would send him off. His father was a doctor, but Allan wasn't bright, and all the kids taunted him he'd end up a garbageman. Not that there weren't worse jobs around, but garbage for Allan was the button, a button that drew fingers like nobody's business. Larry hadn't done that though, all he'd done was claim the fish. They wrestled in the rocks, the algae slime, decaying crayfish and steel-blue mud, even once right over the sucker, probably the crush that did it in. Larry's brother, down the shore, saw the fight and hurried over. Before he got there Allan got a hand free, pulled a pair of Visegrips from his overalls, and made for Larry's eyes. Larry bent his head enough that the plier teeth bit into his brow. Allan raised them for a second go, but stopped, Larry's brother grabbed the arm, and the two of them — his brother and Allan — stiffened dark against the washed-out sky. Allan passed out — Larry was told — and his brother pulled off his own T-shirt, balled it up and stanched the stunning flow of blood from Larry's head. He waved someone over to look to Allan, and biked Larry crossbar all the way home. Larry was worried about the fish. His brother said forget it, the thing was diseased. But Larry, stitched up, returned the next day. It was still there, dead now, grey, deep in flies. He drove the flies off and dug a hole in the heavy clay bank and buried the fish. He covered the broken ground with moss and stuck a branching stick at the head. He wondered a little about fish heaven, what it was like, if all fish went.

"What's up?" says Larry.

"Court date," says Ed. There's a silence. "Thing with re-morse."

The silence this time goes on even longer, till Larry can think of only one question. "What'd you do?" The words ride his breath unwillingly, and scatter on release. Ed takes a moment to gather them in.

"Got caught," he starts, but the bitterness seems to scald his mouth in the saying. "Got bent," he says quietly, "Super Bowl Sunday . . . Hawaiian . . . and no beer shortage. I'd got this letter in the mail the week before, forgot about it, one of those chains, stuffed it away, it was late in the third, I's at my buddy's, one of those ones where if you ignore it your house burns down or your wife leaves or your brother gets killed — I don't know — by lightning. I had off my belt. I'd put on some weight, winter an' all, Jerry had a drill, I was gonna make holes, I was gonna extend the capacity, like, so I could wear it more, the belt. I's sitting there and I couldn't remember if the letter come on a Friday or Monday, I had seven days according to the warning. My feeling, okay, is this — the brain's got all that extra room? nine-tenths or something unused, like an iceberg? So everything you've seen or felt or sensed any way whatsoever, thinking you're only aware of one tenth, and you add up the things you can actually remember, multiply that by nine, it leaves a lot of room for storage. So anyhow I's tryna remember, to access it, right, if I stored that detail. But nothing happened. So I drove home.

To see. Fuck knows. On the way I run a red, hit this Volvo, shook up a family. Did more damage to myself, right, psychologically, which makes sense. But it's when I'm signing over my stuff to the cops — they found half'n ounce in the glove — it's not till then, standing at the counter handing things over one by one, I realise I'm not wearing my belt, my buckle, my Peterbilt is sitting there on the work-mate in Jerry's basement. First time I drove in years without the buckle. So it's like, how did that chain letter know?"

Larry nods, but due to the dark it's lost on Ed, who lights a cigarette. His face seems to climb down into the flame, which then expires, a tiny red ember remaining, a firefly ghosting his chin. The bedsprings sigh.

"Remorse," says Larry.

"Yeah," leaps Ed. "*Showing* remorse. I mean, I can feel some, that's not the problem. It's whether or not — y'know — I can show it."

"I killed a guy with a toaster," says Larry.

Time goes by, he's not sure how long, in the deep dark wandering wait for response.

"Figured as much," Ed finally replies. "Not, y'know, with a toaster, but . . . "

Larry explains, describing the night he'd gone with one of the guys from the warehouse to a party where he knew no one else. One guy there he got talking to said he'd caught a fifty-pound muskie, which was something. Ten minutes later he'd upped it to seventy. Larry informed him the record — to his knowledge — was sixty-seven, and the guy took offence. They were in the kitchen, he pulled a knife, said "You callin' me a liar?" and Larry reached for the only thing available, a two-slice pop-up. The guy came toward him, slipped on some spilt beer, and stumbled, slashing Larry's sleeve before the knife lodged in a cupboard door. It stuck there long enough for Larry to get the toaster cord around the guy's neck. The knife came free, but soon after dropped, and then there was foam leaking out between the teeth. Others came in. The throat was a shambles. Larry wouldn't let go of the toaster until the ambulance people arrived.

"Sixty-seven. Hard to imagine."

"Yeah, and it'll probably stand. Damage to habitat, the key lakes overfished . . . "

"Amen," says Ed. "Amen to that."

The great fish rises in their shared mind's eye, breaks the surface, buckles, returns.

"Ed?"

"Yeah?"

"What'd Madelaine do?"

"Killed two guys . . . with a stove . . . gas." Ed turns heavily toward the wall. "Says they had it coming."

Sirens somewhere far off cry. A flashlight beam crosses Larry's feet, moves to his torso and lingers there. Through slit eyes he watches his own chest rise and fall and rise till the light moves on. The person on rounds sniffs the air, but by now Ed's smoke is well-dispersed. The light goes. Before it returns, the room holds bodies only.

Saturday morning they're left to their own devices whether to get up or not. Larry lies in bed and makes himself weightless. *Prison is a state of mind*. Read that somewhere, read too of the guy on Death Row whom they could not kill until he'd done an IQ test. The doctors encouraged him to try to do well. They needed a sixty in order to execute and he came in with a seventy-two. If he'd got below sixty he'd have been judged too stupid to have known what he was doing when he did what he did. The seventy-two proved otherwise.

Madelaine's voice drifts down the hall. He can't make out the content but she sounds amused. He twists down to the end of the bed, extends himself off it a foot or so, peers out and sees Madelaine and Ed and a fellow from Maintenance who's mounting a mirror. It's a fish-eye, angled to relay back down the hall any movement in the blind spot just in front of the men's washroom door. Ed says something and Madelaine smiles. *Killer smile*, Larry thinks, but then thinks what if he didn't know she'd killed? It's one of those smiles they say light up rooms, she must've had a smile before the murders, would it differ, a smile that came without those facts? She turns her head, she looks down the hall, and Larry ducks back out of view.

Ten minutes later he takes a seat at a servery table, across from Ed. The servery has closed but breakfast debris has yet to be cleared by a hungover student inching along the nausea wire. Madelaine emerges from the kitchen, two plates in hand, and makes her way to their table. She sits, placing the plates between them. On one is a pile of sealed single servings of jam, peanut butter, honey. On the other is toast, fifteen slices, excellently done.

"I could eat a horse," she informs them, slathering the first piece with crimson jam. She nods to the two of them to start on in. Ed does, but Larry hesitates.

Witch, he thinks. The jam on her lips.

She catches his eye, then puts down her toast. "Sorry, that was thoughtless. You want something else? Cereal? Eggs? I can have a look."

Larry is caught off-guard by her sincerity. He turns to Ed, looking for help, and meets instead a sheepish grin.

"We were talking. Sorry. It came up, you know — *how* — like with strategies."

"Question of appearances," Madelaine says. "You're home free, if you want my opinion. You don't attack a man who's holding a knife with a toaster, no one does. You'd only use a toaster defensively. Not like a knife. Not like gas."

Larry gives the hint of a nod, and folds some toast into his mouth. The three of them eat a while in silence.

"I have to prove an ongoing threat. Or my lawyer does," says Madelaine. "It's funny with appearances. Funny-odd."

Her gaze locks in and holds for maybe a minute on the pyramid of toast, as if the answer lay buried within, the answer to this and so much else.

Tania comes in from her afternoon pass, bow-legged, listing a bit to one side, and joins Larry on the couch, from where he's watching golf on TV.

"You like this shit?"

"No," says Larry, more defensively than he'd wish. He picks up a magazine, a *National Geographic*, and opens it at random. It's an article on South Pacific houses built on stilts to survive typhoons.

"Hey," says Tania, "you should get one of those. Fish without even getting out of bed."

Larry smiles. It's a nice thought. He wonders how it would be, sleeping, under your head only water or a breeze. Tania crosses her legs, moans, and puts the crossed one back. Larry looks over and notices a large bruise on the inside of her knee, swollen something fierce.

"What happened?"

"I hit a bike. Walked right into it. Not too swift, huh?" She pauses. Her jaw drops. "Wow, 'magine pulling off that shit?" — this in regard to a chip from a sand-trap thirty feet across the green and into the cup. "Guess though if that's what you do with your life . . . " She takes out a cigarette. They go to commercial.

He thinks of the last time he swung a club. He caddied a lot in his mid-teens but couldn't afford membership fees. Sometimes they'd sneak out in the early morning, before the greens-keepers hit the course. Particular morning he'd dropped his first hole-in-one, five-iron on a short par three. He could've escaped if he'd really wanted. He heard the cart coming, a low rattle hum beneath birds and the sleepless creak of willows, been up all night drinking, he was seventeen, he stood there smirking his face off in the soft dawn, his sneakers soaked in dew, his shirt a sponge for hours of beer, peppermint schnapps, cigarillos and pizza. Stood adrift in the rich rot of grass, the loaded air, one hand loose on the iron's grip, the other stroking mist up off his face and into his trembling hair, his eyes still fixed on the cut in space only now closing on the ball's perfect fall. The cart pulled up, the keepers got out, two college guys with expensive muscles, they escorted him off with the invitation not to return, or face charges. He asked them could he retrieve his ball. They asked where it was. He told them. They laughed and said to piss off before they called the cops. It ended up he did return, again early morning, the same par three, with a friend in the friend's high-traction pickup. Drunk, they did a donut on the green. After a rain. Serious glazed. The hole was closed for a couple of weeks, the time it took for the new grass to set. Word had it the members were annoyed, some suggested electric fences, some wanted all-night armed guards. Larry quit. It wasn't worth the risk, specially with those college guys around. His last swing was a moment of grace. No one else saw it. Maybe why.

"Earth to Larry."

He searches out the source. It's Gavin, sitting at a table nearby, looking for a euchre fourth.

Tania grinds out her cigarette. "Ignore him like the plague," she mutters, gets up and crosses out of the room, favouring the bruised knee.

"Larry, how 'bout it?" comes Ed's voice.

Larry gets up and wanders over, stands to one side as he considers.

"What's with her?" Gavin adds, "with the walk."

Larry shrugs.

Gavin rocks on the rear legs of his chair, his toes only barely keeping contact with the floor.

"Meds," Ed suggests.

"Nah," says Gavin. "Must've had work done, chowder-hole tightened . . . "

Larry watches Gavin's hands, the long thin fingers with the blur of cards between them. He doesn't bother with Gavin's face. His foot swings out soccer-style and meets the leg of the tilting chair. Things like that — what happens to time — Gavin, mouth open but nothing to say, seeming almost frozen in recline. But then he begins to drop back. His hands reach out but there's nothing to grab, the cards burst up like spooked birds, his body stiffens awaiting the floor. First, though, his head — the back of the skull, just where the skull meets the nape of the neck — catches the rim of a heavy stonework pot containing an ancient aspidistra. The head snaps forward, the body continues down through the last few inches to the floor. Breathing goes on, but little else. Blood appears where the tip of the tongue protrudes through a break in the hammered grin. Larry looks down at the bright chest. *Life's a Beach*, the T-shirt reads. Larry's gaze wanders back and up to Ed, several steps from him, staring at the body. In his hand Ed holds the buckle, fingers it as if for clues.

Larry lies in bed, his hands a little church rising from his chest. Minutes throb through him like a wound. He's watched the feet of Sam, the staff-guy sitting with him, for some time. Soon the doorway feet should change. He's wondering how they got that sturgeon in the truck. Eight hundred pounds, you'd need a hoist. Something. They must've gone looking for the fish, knowing it was out there, they'd have had to have a plan.

Madelaine's face appears at the door, hovers strangely, lit from below. There is no movement on Sam's part, and it's then Larry notices the gentle drone. Madelaine squeezes partway in and peers into the dark for Larry.

"Hi," he whispers, so she can place him.

"Hi. Thought you might like to know . . . hospital called . . . apparently he's conscious."

Larry breathes out, from every pore.

"Better for you I guess. Even so . . . " Dangling from her finger is the key to the servery, something — past midnight — she's not supposed to have. "Want some toast?"

Whether due to the light or the water in his eyes, her half-smile holds him like a spell. He shrugs but it soon wanders into a nod. Madelaine goes. Larry lies back, takes from his desk the Shakespeare reel, winds it and winds it, and, on the rhythmic drone from Sam, he drifts.

White like before, but clearer, like ice. Muffled thunder. He holds a putter, but can't see the ball or even the hole. It isn't

cold, only white. A crack appears in the ice, a yawn. Dark
water spouts, then washes over. Up to the hole this grey thing
comes rising — grey-blue-green — then breaks the surface.
It's a muskellunge, twenty feet long, leaping, but it stops at
the top of the leap, hangs there, fixed, pulsing in the sky.
Gradually it sinks and settles on the ice. Larry approaches. It
rolls on its back like a puppy and Larry strokes its velvet
belly. It makes a noise, a happy groan, then slips back through
the hole in the ice. Larry wipes his hand down his arm and
sees that his hand is trailing silver — filaments of eggs — all
over his clothes, and the eggs turn to glittering silver scale.
He stands there in his silver scale suit, it fits like a glove, he
opens his mouth and the voice coming out is Elvis Presley's
twisted into his. He turns and sees Giselle Lavoie from high
school coming through tall grass toward him. She says, "I
didn't know you could sing." She becomes the nurse who
asked him his dreams. They kiss. He wonders if he should
ask her about her clothes, if she'd be willing. He doesn't
want to make it any more awkward than it is — or isn't yet,
but could be, later, when they talk.

TANGO

- Our cat disappeared.
- That's not how it started. That was like the culmination.
- Enough is enough you say to yourself.
- We did.
- I think it's pretty standard. [*pause*] Mind if I smoke?
- That was the escalation — with the cat. Culminating in what occurred.
- Day One . . . you want my opinion.
- We sensed stuff immediate. Day they pulled in. A Honda?
- Tercel. '81 hatch. Not bad shape considering the age.
- I think you could say . . . we had our *suspicions*. I looked in the mirror . . .
- Thereabouts.
- Point is I could hardly believe my eyes. The eyes especially, around the sockets, grey, the strain . . .
- Tried this paste. Cream.
- Vitamin E, but even so. It gets to the point when you really must realize . . .
- Might have to draw a line.

- We don't mind music. We're not *against* it. Depending, you know.
- Play some ourselves.
- We dance. Or did. Not so much now. There's not the oppor-tunities, and what with Keith's knees. Used to dance till I

blistered, remember? We'd go out, I'd have to bring a box of Band-Aids.

- Wasn't the first time I wandered over. Second, I think . . . April?
- April.
- Ground was pret-near thawed up. He'd weasled this culti-vator from Mackinnon. Mackinnon lent 'im it, don't ask me why. Mackinnon's the sort would cut off his hand for an absolute stranger. Then not even bother to ask for it back.
- Decent but easily . . . easily *swayed*.
- I heard the shrieking. Fellow was driving the bejesus out of it, up and over rock, brush, could hear the blades shrieking a good hundred yard. Got on my boots, still fairly swamp the stretch between the properties where there's the run-off.
- A *maze*. You give the idea some thought.
- Hay there two years back, then it got sold, went fallow, but nothing much to hold it. Then the rains. Then — there-abouts — is when they came. Fall last.
- November.
- November.
- I remember it was two days past Remembrance.
- But this was April, day I went over. [*pause*] Sure you don't mind? [*pause*] Interduced myself.
- Hard to believe, even now. And I've seen some strangeness in this life.
- I'll tell you he had this path staked out. Lines. To try to figure the con . . .
- . . . figuration.
- Configuration, how he had it. Squares inside squares with rectangles, triangles, thing — what you call it . . .
- Rhombus.
- A rhombus.

- [*blush*] Grade Ten geometry.
- This Bob-fellow's driving a groove through mud . . .
- Intending to.
- . . . in the shape of a rhombus. Diamond-shape. Asked him what he was thinking to grow. [*pause*] Trees, he told me. Shrubbery.
- Saints preserve us.
- Shrubbery. [*coughs*]
- He'd quit you know. Nearly entirely. But what with the disturbances, the aggravation . . .
- Could be worse.
- . . . but I say twice is only one more time than once.
- Four packs a day . . . one point in time.
- I said — enough. Even just financially. The taxes. Ashtray's a government donation box.
- Thought of growing my own. I did. Crossed my mind.
- Over my dead body.
- Promises, promises . . . [*chuckle, pause*] Anyhow.
- In the field.
- I was in the field. Takes off his hat. Old battered wide-brim felt type, brown with some sorta feather . . .
- Crow.
- . . . in the band. Hair pulled up in a pony-tail, sticking out the top of his head. Each his own.
- Matter of opinion.
- Wiped his brow with a red and white rag you wouldn't choke a dog with. Shrubbery huh? I say to 'im. That, or a drive-in, he goes. I look him over up and down, and then he starts smirking to beat the band. Let him know I'd never much had a leaning to having my chain tugged. Smirk goes away. Week or so later I'm down at Mackinnon's. I say, have you seen what that Bob-fellow's doing? Fellow you loant that cultivator to? He says no, that it probably

wouldn't be much to look at for some time yet. Growing a labyrinth takes some patience, is what he tells me, to grow a good labyrinth.

- Maze.
- A maze made out of trees. He was getting the ground ready for seedlings, to put in seedlings — poplar . . .
- Poplar!
- . . . he says for rapid definition, followed by yew, juniper, so on. Field next to ours, no questions asked. [pause] If I'm recollecting correctly . . .
- Go on, honey.
- . . . he asked me did I know of other property about.
- For sale.
- Now, he may have seen my name. On some sign — I've been in the trade. I'm not that active. We lost our broker. Or didn't lose him. He left, moved to Florida. Something with his joints.
- Arizona.
- Was it Arizona?
- Wouldn't be Florida. Florida's humid. If it was his joints.
- So . . . [pause] He left, and the four of us . . . us with our licences — they aren't much good if you don't have a broker, registered — so in a sense I guess you could say I was lying fallow. Real-estate-wise.
- We manage.
- The thing was, I thought who's this fellow wandering in, holes in his pants, asking if there's any more land t'acquire.
- Before you know it, see it happen, you're basically an island in a sea of cranks.
- Bushes, you know, I can see the place of bushes.
- Front lawns, patios.
- Trees have their role.

- But here was this eminent tourist attraction.
- Or park.
- There's no prize for being naïve.

- Hardly saw them over the winter.
- Once or twice, at a distance. You'd see the lights. Go on or off. Some days the car was gone, some days there.
- Small community. No one else . . .
- Wouldn't see them go, or come. Mail'd arrive under four different names. I asked our driver. Just in passing.
- Hide nor hair.
- Like aliases.
- "Low profile" — that the term?
- Seen that show — "America's Most Wanted"?
- Then one day they left the car-lights on. Still below zero. I figured, with the battery . . .
- So Keith went over.
- Seemed the decent thing. [*pause*] Took a look in, was about to knock. [*pause*] She come down the stairs with nothing on but a pair of cut-off jeans. I knocked. Just so's of course they wouldn't think . . .
- What he was doing there, on their porch.
- Came to the door she had on a shirt.
- Man's.
- The fellow's. She said hello.
- Prominent bosom.
- I mentioned the lights, said I'd turn 'em off if she had the keys, or if it was open, save her the walk. She said she thought it oughta be open. I said fine, I'd have a look. She asked did I want to come in. For coffee.
- Shirt and shorts. Nothing underneath.

- I said I didn't drink coffee after breakfast. Interduced my-self. She invited me in. [*pause*] I stayed put. Stayed at the door.
- But got a look.
- I got a look in. [*pause*] Pretty untidy, but besides that.
- You said a mess.
- There was lots of stuff scattered. Like they'd only just moved in.
- Been there four months. This was late March. They still hadn't happened to unpack their boxes.
- Or maybe they were packing.
- They didn't leave.
- No. True.
- They stayed where they were.

- Looked over one day. This was May. Two in the afternoon. Smoke pouring out the chimney like a house on fire. Black. I said to Keith — look at that smoke.
- It was pretty black.
- Remember I said . . .
- I thought maybe — who knows — a dirty oil burner.
- Keith.
- All right. I said it was black.
- A few days later? I passed her in town. Mentioned we'd happened to see the smoke. She guessed who I was. I didn't have to say. She said she'd seen me out in the yard. She forced a sort of pastry on me. Made it herself. It was very sweet. Oily, nuts and honey and pastry like skin that flakes off after a sunburn? I noticed, the next day, flaws in my complexion.
- Can't rule out the pork.

- It was not the pork. Why you maintain . . . [*pause*] I have
  no aversion reaction to pork. [*pause*] Pork agrees with me.
- It's only, y'know . . .
- Honey.
[*silence*]
- Mind if I smoke?
- I don't want to sound *disappointed* in people. I don't want
  to give the sense that we were fed up with people — *in
  general*, you know? [*pause*] Things, you could say, went
  from bad to worse. Some days I'd get up, I'd have no colour. Pale as paste. No colour at all . . .
- To speak of.
- . . . in my facial features. My hair lost its sheen. I felt fatigued.
  I felt . . . [*pause*] even Keith . . . distant.
- I . . .
- No one can tell me what I did or did not feel. [*pause*] He
  hadn't those plants in the ground a month . . .
- Bob.
- . . . and you could see the growth. Green. Almost pulsing.
  Rows of green. Those patterns, feeding off the surround-
  ings. Ground round here is rich in nutrition, magnetism . . .
  [*pause*] Or I'd be in town. I'd drop by Nature's Bounty,
  for instance? and what did I find — her pastries, her muf-
  fins, on their very own rack. Selling like hotcakes.
- Tasted okay.
- Oh, they tasted fine! How does it go — "some sugar on the
  bullet"? [*pause*] Keith seemed to think that she was the innocent, the one led down the garden path.
- What I said . . .
- It was *her* bloody garden! He looked after the labyrinth
  business but she was the one in the garden.
- All right! [*pause*] She wore a cross . . . all I was meaning . . .

- Blasphemy.
- Seems to me you can't wear a cross and not have it some-how affect you.
- Besides, it wasn't a *cross* cross. It was one of those . . . pagan prehistorical . . . with hooks and a snaking thing over the crossbar.
- People get led astray, is all . . .
- Grant me patience.
- I'm not saying him. Him I spoke to. I spoke to about it. Scripture and such. Asked had he read any Road to *Forever,* any *Witness to Wonder,* or *Dreaming the Supreme.* I coulda been talking to a brick wall. He said it wasn't his sort of thing. I asked what was. Plants, he said. He said he believed in plants.
- Don't they all.
- I'm sorry, honey, it's been . . . you know . . . but when he said . . . with God and weeds, that God was there as much in a weed as a flower, that pesticides were evil, and heaven . . . heaven was crabgrass and thistle and skunk cabbage sprouting up out of the brains of the dead . . .
- Keith's usually cool as a cucumber.
- Came that close. [*finger-thumb gesture*] What I said was obviously we were coming from pretty different places. He agreed. He wasn't stupid. I give him that. He was not stupid.
- To my mind one's as guilty as the other. It's symbiotic. It's a partnership. I don't believe in this *woman as victim.* I say this as a woman. She knew where she stood.

- You draw the line somewhere. Some point you say — enough. Good if you know ahead of time where it is exactly you see that line drawn, just so later . . .

- We drew ours together.
- . . . however you've drawn it, once you've drawn it, you're ready to stand by it, come whatever.
- Hell or high water.
- You draw one or you don't.
- That's our feeling.
- Long as you make the understanding clear. That they understand how you're situated, at what point what's asking too much.
- Perhaps we weren't as clear as we could've . . . *been*.
- They'd have had to be nuts.
- Nuts, dumb, or malicious — I think that's pretty much the total gamut.
- I'm not saying stand over the line. Threaten.
- Point fingers.
- Provoke. [*pause*] Just if what you'd thought was clear is not . . .
- Is vague.
- . . . on where you stand . . .
- Where you stand firm.
- . . . one day you wake up and the line you'd thought you'd drawn is gone . . .
- Erased.
- . . . or crossed over . . .
- Erased in the night.
- . . . well, then you've got a problem. [*pause*] The morning I got up and Meowsy . . .
- Our cat.
- . . . our cat Meowsy wasn't there, at the window, to get let in . . .
- Keith came and told me, asked had I seen Meowsy, well of course I hadn't, I was still in bed. The cat — we don't let her into the bedroom. Didn't. I'm allergic. Not all the

93

time, just so long as she keeps a certain distance, doesn't sleep on my face and stuff. She likes to crawl up under my chin. Be sleeping, I'd wake with hair in my mouth. It got, you know, a little much. [*pause*] Keith she doesn't bother, not to that degree.

- We have an understanding.
- [*smile*] Keith was the "bad cop." [*pause*] Her hair, if you brush her, her hair's so light it *floats upward*, you watch it with the sun coming in, the filaments actually seem to go up.
- She wasn't there when I went down for coffee.
- Saturdays, Keith puts the coffee on. We had a machine, one with a timer, but it gave out — what, one week past warranty?
- Par for the course.
- He's an early bird anyhow. I don't think he minds. Besides, it's nice for me.
- I sensed something . . .
- You know how you *know* things?
- I didn't know *what* exactly, but I knew . . .
- He's got an intuition.
- Honey.
- It's true.
- I got on my boots and I stepped out on the drive — it was raining I remember — and I whistled.
- She'd come when you whistle. Not all cats do.
- That's when I went back up and asked Viv.
- Had I seen her, and of course I hadn't.
- Spent the better part of the day wandering the field, calling out. Evening came we were at our wit's end.
- That's when I said perhaps we should ask them.
- I thought maybe a truck, or even a fox, we'd had one around, I'd seen tracks.

- I said perhaps we should take a walk over.
- I got out the gun. Thought if I saw the fox, not thinking . . .
  just to scare the thing off.
- We'd heard the music before on weekends. It carries.
- You know, and you know when you're tired?
- I thought we'll just put the question to them, that'd be that,
  and put our minds at rest.
- Bugs were bad. We got eaten alive.
- We could see their silhouettes, even from the driveway.
- Sun'd gone down.
- We could see them dancing. The light was weird. Candles
  all over.
- The windows were open.
- I said to Keith, they don't look dressed.
- We were still a ways off, still calling to Meowsy.
- But over their music . . .
- . . . losing battle. I thought you know if I fired a shot. Get
  their attention.
- So Keith fired the once.
- Reloaded out of habit.
- They came to the window. Their silhouettes . . .
- . . . like. So we wandered up. The door was open but we
  knocked anyways. I called, shouted his name — Bob.
- The hallway — you know the way candles flicker? and with
  the wind that was blowing through that house . . .
- Moths like crazy bouncing off the walls . . .
- They'd been dancing I think.
- Close.
- That's not what you said.
- I said . . .
- Like standing-up sex.
- Eerie, besides that. Noise and the light . . .
- So we took a step in.

- Everywhere paintings . . .
- . . . hanging on the walls and leaning on furniture.
- Lots of black and grey and stuff . . .
- Mono-chromo.
- . . . but most like the paint had just been thrown, like he'd put on a blindfold or something and flung it . . .
- Or she had.
- No sure way to know. [*pause*] Stare at those things long enough you could start to see shapes, faces pret-near.
- I didn't see faces.
- Depend on the angle.
- The noise was unbelievable. And then I saw something run beneath a chair.
- She came out first from the next room back. Had on a under-shirt . . .
- . . . and pair of panties. Sweating like mad. She yelled his name — Bob.
- I yelled to her we were looking for our cat.
- Her eyes were glazed.
- Stunned like. [*pause*] Then he comes up from behind the couch where they got their tapes and records stored. He'd got on a pair of jeans I guess . . .
- When they must've seen us.
- Anyhow. [*pause*] So the two of them stood there staring at us, like we were aliens from Mars or something. He looked at the gun. I wasn't holding it up or nothing, it wasn't even cocked.
- All of a sudden he dives for the fireplace.
- And she run off back toward the kitchen.
- He turns around and he's got from the firedog an iron poker and it's over his head . . .
- He's heading our way . . .

- . . . and I screamed to Keith . . .
- Had to once drop a moose that distance, but that time I had some trees between us. This time I get it up and fire, from the hip, meaning to slow 'im, make him drop the poker, whatever. [*pause*] Buckshot though, it makes an impression.
- Then I see her coming down the hall and she's got this Chinese cleaver in her hand. Keith's further in and she goes for him. His back is turned but I guess he saw something cause he twists to one side and she tumbles right over him. I see the Bob-fellow's poker on the floor, right where he dropped it, between where they're tumbled. The gun goes off into the couch . . .
- Accidental.
- . . . and I realise Keith's got no more cartridges at the ready. He's on his stomach with the gun underneath like a sitting duck and she's getting up. She's gashed herself on the arm with the cleaver, blood's coming out, and you know it only makes her look madder . . .
- Mad like insane.
- I think, okay girl, it's your husband or your neighbour. Making the actual decision wasn't hard. Things she was screaming would make a sailor blush.
- Viv picks up the poker and sticks it out, square in the path of Bob's wife. Gets her I guess in the middle of the chest?
- I don't know what I thought she'd do . . . when the poker went in . . . how she'd react.
- Stood there a minute before she dropped.
- Not a minute.
- Okay. Seconds.
- I know it sounds kooky . . . but maybe for an instant? I thought . . . well . . . what if she bursts into flames.

- Too many movies.
- I-know-I-know . . . but with the light, and her eyes all glassy, glowing, I thought, there's always a first time, you never know . . .
- Anyhow. [*pause*] So the two of them lay there.
- Completely misunderstood why we'd come.
- We called the police. Realized we had to. We could've if we wanted just burnt the place down.
- Five minutes probably I was blowing out candles. We turned on the lights, turned on every light.
- Police, you know, they put me on hold. I called the wrong number. I didn't dial Emergency. I dialed I guess the reception desk. [*pause*] Thing is it didn't feel like an Emergency, by that point.
- After the fact.
- Told them they could find us back at the house. They said they didn't want us leaving the premises. I said hell it's a hop and a skip. And Viv was starting to feel kinda nauseous.
- You don't like being sick in someone else's house.
- Strange part is, you know what happened? We almost got stuck in Bob's darn maze. I mean, we were there, we could see our own house, we could see the lights on the road into town, but the moon wasn't out and the ground like pitch and we kept stumbling into this knee-high wire. I'd say we must've been a good fifteen minutes just trying to find our way out of that thing. Hardly'd we even got to our porch 'fore we saw the cop-car lights coming.
- And sitting there, pretty as you please . . .
- Sitting on our porch was our cat Meowsy. Where she'd been . . .
- We can only guess.

- It's difficult. [*pause*] With the time we might be gone . . .
- It's give her away or have her put down.
- Don't know anyone who wants a cat?
- Hate to have her land up in the wrong hands. You know?

NICKEL & DIME

Couple summers back I spent a fair bit of time with Basil drinking after work when we both were on road crew doing repairs for this outfit the dad of a guy we knew from high school ran. We raked and did flags and Basil was planning the next year to take the bulldozer course. We'd played together the winter before on the district champs, we had that in common, but not everyone you get to know, even when you're on the same team. The summer went fast, by in a blur, nights out drinking and days in the sun. We done one overnight in the clink, too many beers, we snuck up on some cows asleep and pushed them over, laughed enough to wake the dead — but first the farmer, who called the cops.

That October Basil's buddy Jack bought it playing chicken, and Basil took off to the west coast. I'd heard he come back, but that was all till the one night I was working Donny's car wash, and who pulls up but Basil in this Trans-Am. His buddy Jack died in a Trans, exact same colour, stripes and all. Every time one of them goes by I think for a sec — there goes a ghost. Things you don't know, nobody does. Then seeing Basil the guy getting out. He goes to me *where's the fire?* like always, we have some muds since the car wash is dead and he pulls a mickey from the glove, tops us up which is okay with me 'cause Donny was gone, he'd left me the keys to close, and so long as I didn't ruin my judgement. Basil hoist his feet till closing, then we drank and drove around till I woke up on his couch the next morning. His sister Elise go by in her bathrobe, look me over, I see with the one eye that opens, she sits in the rocker, the sun's crawling down the couch at me, and I got up and made it at least to the toilet before everything from the night before come back up with a vengeance. After a while there's a knocking on the door, Elise voice going *it's for you*. I try to say something but my words bounce around in the toilet bowl instead of coming out, it's disorientating, and I vomit some more. When I'm empty and cleaned up and standing I go out and both of them are sitting on the couch like nothing's the matter, Elise watching *Newsworld* and Basil eating scrambled eggs. Elise say hi and there's coffee on the stove. Also it was Donny on the phone and I left the place unlocked and he wants back the keys. Basil calls Donny a *capitalist dog*, looks at Elise, and raises his eyebrows. Elise say if Basil had brains he'd be dangerous, then goes gets me coffee, probably since I don't move. Basil give me a look like he's getting her goat, but I'm too sick to figure out how.

Donny was willing to keep me on, but part-time supervised and with a cut in pay. Basil was with me, he'd drove me in, said *screw that noise* in Donny's earshot. Donny asked who was speaking for me. I said I'd have to think. He said so long as I didn't think too long. We went to the liquor store and Basil stocked up. I said *what's the occasion*? He goes *we're free men*.

It was first week October, and Elise headed back that day to college off the Island, their parents had gone to winter in Florida two weeks before, so the place was his. Or *ours*, since Basil said I could crash. They lived a quarter mile off the pave, old farm-place his Dad had worked, then rented off the pasture to neighbours. There was lots of food in the freezer from their garden, more in the garden, and lots of cans, and at the bottom of the freezer a pig. Or half a pig, in sections.

This meant we hardly had to go out, except to the village store for smokes or milk or eggs or what-have-you, videos. I never lived on a farm before so the whole thing was new, like an education.

One day something went all sour. We'd set to drinking by eleven in the morning, rum in the coffee and on from there, and Basil just got blacker by the hour. By mid-afternoon I left him alone, took a bottle up on the roof and watched the clouds, and the sun on the sea. Basil went out back and I heard this banging and creaking and general noise. I looked up over the roof-top ridge and Basil was pulling down a old chicken coop and throwing the lumber in a pile nearby. He didn't seem drunk, he just seem determined, so I guessed it was like a household chore his Mom or Dad had left him to do. I went down and lent a hand. The work went fast, like no time flat. I asked him was there anything else. He sat on a stump and stared at the pile, he had a bottle between his boots but was hardly drinking, he just said *wait*.

By the time it got dusk I was in the kitchen making some corned beef sandwiches and cooking up some veggies I'd pulled from the garden. I had real earth stuck under my nails and blisters on my hands from the wood, the sea wind was coming down the hall from the front, I felt pretty good I'd have to say. Then the wind changed, and it came in the side, with it smoke and the crackle-pop of barnboard. I go to look and see from the kitchen Basil, where he was on his stump, wrapped in himself, rocking and whining and staring into the fire-pile. His lips open maybe half an inch, his teeth closed, his eyes some strange. Whine coming out, a high insect noise, only pausing when he had to breathe. I thought maybe the guy needs food. I got the sandwiches and brought them out and the noise was gone, except for the fire, the tide-roar coming in on the breeze, and Basil whistling "Born to be Wild."

He smiled on and off all the way through the sandwiches, and with the booze the time went by. Basil'd go off every couple minutes and come back with more wood to throw on the fire. It was getting some serious. I rolled back my stump, got steaming slugs between my fingers. I went inside to wash them off. I never liked slugs, their glue-slime. The water pressure in the tap as I run it I realise is not that incredible. And if the sucker got out of hand. I'm thinking this as I step back outside and see Basil standing head to head with flames. Looks like his actual face is cooking. Turns out I don't even have to speak, a car pulls up, it's a guy from the volunteer fire department, he seen the flames from the shore road and thought he better mention some caution. Basil don't respond. The guy's about to get back in his car when Basil picks up another board. The guy come back over and take the board from Basil's hand and Basil lets him. The guy looks at me, says *hose that thing down*. His eyes are black, he's got the muscles for pushing over *wide-awake* cows. I tell him *good idea*. He says *it's not a suggestion*. When it's down to embers the car pulls away. Basil's curled up into the heat. I go get a beer and bring back blankets. It's not a complaint, but whenever I try to talk I get nothing back from him. It's when you think you known someone then realize they're maybe stranger than ever.

Basil the next couple days is fine. Elise call to say she's coming on the weekend, Thanksgiving, and for Basil to pick up a bird. Basil asks what's wrong with pig. She says *nothing, but turkey's traditional*. Basil don't give a hoot for tradition. It comes out she's bringing a friend.

My Dad's in a home for the senile, my Ma crossed the big pond a few years back, my brothers are out west, we weren't raised religious. But whatever Basil thought Thanksgiving meant to me, it was piles more than what it meant to him. He

throws me the keys to the Trans-Am, says *go get a turkey*. I
ask what kind. *Big* he goes. And that was that.

So I got to town and the only damage was to some ducks
off McGoogan's sideroad, they were waddling the incline
from dirt to the pave when I blew by and laid on the horn, I
figured to save them a few duck years, and one or two
flapped into my path, and I had to continue, you can't brake
for ducks. I think I popped one with the antenna, I saw in the
rear-view mirror this spinning bundle of whiteness that
landed in the ditch. I got to town and checked the antenna
for blood, but there wasn't, there was only a couple feathers
stuck in the radiator grill. I went to the bank machine, took
out the last of my cash, and remembered I didn't have a job. I
thought, okay Monday first thing I'll start looking.

I head back to Basil's with booze and the turkey. He was
down at the shore, I knew, loading up the pickup with seaweed to bank the house. I'd told him I'd help soon as I was
back. Parked in the driveway there's a car I don't know,
there'd been letters in the mail for Basil from the courthouse,
for unpaid tickets and I thought, maybe one of those guys in
green cars they send around. It was green all right, but three
different shades. Getting closer I see bumper stickers — a
rubber-booter's Lada, the body falling off. I park and get out
and walk toward the porch. There's a guy sitting there with
his feet against the post. He's wearing moccasins, got in his
mouth a flute-type thing with a feather he's playing. Not the
feather, the feather's just hanging. I'm thinking, not a burglar,
least not a salesman. I try to catch his eye when I walk toward the house, but he's concentrating. Shanty or something.
I see Elise in the window, which explains it, she waves and I
head direct for the door. I open the screen and I'm starting in
when the moccasin guy says *afternoon*. I look back and nod.
He says what sounds like *oooly-eem*, like when you're a kid

and you break words in half and put the back part at the front, but *eem-oooly* don't make any more sense. I nod again and he goes back to playing and I go inside. Elise least I know.

We talk, she talks about mainly school, stuff she's taking, she's in politics and English. She mentions Bill, the guy on the porch. We talk about Basil, she's a little bit worried, him not working, and how his moods go pretty low this time of year. Long as he keeps busy, we decide, and the idea's I keep an eye out. I'd jump in the lake if she asked me, that's the problem. Since Grade Eight I would've and still. But Elise never went with guys from the Island, *gene pool's too small* she said, *in case of accidents*. I remember the conversation, Grade Twelve, I only knew Basil sort of at a distance, I was thinking of asking Elise to the winter prom. I asked her if she was thinking of going. She said no, besides she was dating this college exchange student from Peru. She left school late in the year, left the Island, and most of us wondered whether not some accident'd happened.

I look up and notice Basil back, out on the porch talking with Bill. He sees me through the window and calls for a beer. I take out three. Basil interduces us, but as he says *Bill* Bill says *Oooly-eem*, like before, and we both just stare. But Basil remembers something and gives himself a big fake slap on the forehead. *Sorry* he goes, *sorry sorry*. And says how *Ooolyeem* is old-style for *Bill*. *Gaelic* says Bill, *U—i—l . . .*, and Basil says — *yeah, we get the picture*. Bill — Uilleem — wasn't that bad a guy but he had to know everything. What was the best sort of seaweed for banking, what was the engine displacement on the truck, the beer — he'd never had this beer, and wanted to know the process it was made by. Basil and me, we didn't have a clue. In a vat, I figured. Basil said tanks. *Tanks?* Bill asked him. Basil said *big ones*.

The turkey we ate the following day, long with lots of stuff from the garden — squash, turnip, beets, spuds. Bill went off for a drive in the morning, come back with a basket of wild cranberries. No one could figure out where he got them, and Elise just say *he's a fountain of knowledge*. Things that'd make her go for a guy you could not predict. Not at all.

Dinner went good. We all filled up and afterward Elise brought out some smoke. We sat on the porch and looked at the stars. Bill played some stuff on a mandolin. Basil told stories, funny ones, of travelling. Elise got on her politics kick. Everything she said was true, how a handful of families controlled the country, big buck clans ruling the roost. She got on the Irvings, all the shit they had, she went on and on, and the thing was she meant it. I look over one point, there's tears in her eyes, how no one — anyone — should get to *own* land. Came this long silence. Then Basil say soft — *bastards rob us . . . we should rob 'em back*.

Elise and Bill left on the Monday, after I done a check on the Lada. They said they heard noises. You can't ignore noises is what I told 'em when they asked. Bill gave me a rock he said was good for headaches, you hold it to your head where the pain most is. I told him thanks, I didn't know what else. Elise kissed me, asked me again to keep an eye on Basil in case of an *episode*. First time I'd heard her call them that, and can't say I was keen on the word.

Late that week a guy come round, evangelist, and Basil answers. Mid-afternoon and we're still rough from the night before, celebrating nothing. Basil looks the guy up and down while the guy talks, coming round to what Basil hopes from *the world to come*. Basil's eyes keep moving all over. Me, I'm thinking, is this like the start? But the guy keeps on, he's a selling machine, says he's got a series of pamphlets, little books that *bring the question home*. Basil asks *what question's that*? Why we're here, the guy explains. *On this planet*? Basil asks. *Alive* says the guy. *We're not* says Basil. I get this sudden thing to pee, so go to the toilet and when I come back the evangelist's out by his car, getting in. The driveway's narrow and swings behind the house and continues out the other side, but this guy whatever reason decides to back all the way, the way he come in, he keeps looking back at the house and each time he does he nearly ditches the car. I'm about to crack up, but Basil turning, his eyes are mean. *More things under heaven and earth* is all he say when he shuffle by.

Week later I'm down to nickels and dimes, and for me that's always the sign. I tell Basil I gotta get work. I don't say he does, it's his house, though I'd been covering past my share. Basil says *relax*. The last couple days he'd spent sitting alone a lot by the fire-pit. He didn't do anything outright strange, but this drinking for a living, it was taking its toll. Basil said Monday — Mondays were best. He had enough tucked away to last us over any emergency. He knew about a party — Hallowe'en — on the weekend, people he knew would be at, people who'd know about some work. He goes *relax, we're dust in the wind*. Meaning like the song.

Saturday came, we were driving to town, just after supper, dark out but not as dark as it would be the week next, daylight saving time on top of everything else. Colder too, we had on our hockey jackets, Basil'd thrown me mine at the door, said — *hey, Nob!* — which was a joke since when they sewed my name on the jacket they screwed up and put a *N* where the *B* was s'posed to be. I missed the deadline for bringing back flaws, I magic-markered the triangles closed, but first time I washed it the marker came out. So I kept it, nobody calls me that, 'cept for guys from the team, guys I see maybe once in a dog's age. I was driving, Basil let me. We're halfway to town when he throws in my lap a nylon — *put it on* he says. I go *what's this*? He says *we're going as robbers*. I ask where's the party. He gives directions, out the other end of Airport Road. He pulls a twenty-sixer from under the seat, has a swig, then hands me it. I do the same. Looking down I see the gas gauge light's come on. We pass an Esso, then a Shell. We go past an Ultramar. He waves me on. I tell him he thinks I'm gonna push he might as well forget it. An Irving comes up and I look to Basil and he gives this shrug like it's my decision. I pull in. There's no one else around. Basil puts his hand in his pocket and pulls out this real-looking plastic gun. *Fill'er up regular* he says and tucks it back in his jacket and then gets out. He pulls down his nylon, his back's to the attendant who's walking from the station out to the booth. Just as the guy gets the key in the lock, Basil wheels and forces him in. I see him shove the guy up against the glass, see the guy's face flattened, held there, blinking. I want to tell him the gun's not real, just so's he knows he's not about to die. It hits me we're going nowhere without gas, so I get out and put the nozzle in. I'm watching the numbers spin on dial, my hand goes numb, then jerks, and gas spurts out across the side of the car — if there's one good thing the good thing here would be nobody's smoking, that'd be it. Then I hear Basil yelling at me, he's at the booth door, gun pointed at my head — my nylon I forgot about. I pull it down but can't then read the gas gauge numbers, but it doesn't matter. Basil says *get in the car*, and we do. The guy pops up, the guy in the booth, his head, like at the midway or something, and Basil turns and aims right at him. The guy drops. He must've forgot the glass is s'posed to be bullet-proof.

We're pulling away and I think did I screw the gas-cap on, and almost stop — but don't, I just drive, I drive us home.

I'm at the kitchen table rolling the coins. Basil wouldn't say how much in bills, but I guess it wasn't what he hoped. He's out back burning the evidence, the nylons and gun, and getting a tarp across the car till we get it repainted. I suddenly know who the booth guy was — Belanger's cousin from up eastern end. I played him in juvenile finals way back. Belanger noses do this thing, they spread out just before they meet the forehead, their eyes look buried in their head, but none of them I ever seen wore glasses. I look at my jacket sitting on the chair. I think about Basil's he's still got on. Number 4. Number 11. I've done the nickels, the pennies and dimes, I'm trying not to think, I start on the quarters, I take a long swig off the bottle on the table, and putting my head back I see, on the ceiling, lights running window patterns across it. First I think the fire, the light from the burning, but it's steadier than that, and then there's the megaphone. ZZTop I had on loud, I had to turn down in order to hear. I get up to go to the stereo and meet a guy with a gun on my head. He says something, and I do what he says which I think is *lie face-down on the floor*. That's at least where I end up, where I am when they put on the cuffs.

Driving to town Basil's calmer than the dead. I watch him to make sure he's breathing. They told us we had the right to be quiet, everything out of our mouths could be used. This point I'm too mad to care. I ask him what the hell was he thinking. My brain starts throbbing into my eyes. He don't respond. I think of Bill's rock in my pocket I can't reach because of the cuffs. We go a few miles like that, we're coming into town, when Basil's head locks on something and turns. I look back and recognize the building where Jack, his dead buddy, used to live. He says real soft *I loved that guy.* It's when someone says a thing that wasn't obvious till after they said it. *I know* I tell him, pretending I did. Whatever that makes me, a liar or what.

Vegetative symptoms someone was saying (I overheard) were a concern. In-law of some sort or other. I was in the office. It was just in passing. Vegetable land, you give it some thought. Vitamins, minerals. When this sort of thing becomes even less than scribbling, that I was an actual man at one time. Things most like memories that flicker and fade, not however with any detail by which you might firmly grasp them as yours, as from your life, your own. More like a movie, or dream (of course), but a dream you've no recollection having had, someone else's, or someone else's memory, which leaked out, which you've accidentally come across, which sticks to the brain like shit to a shoe. You'd think whatever memories you have would come at least from your own experience. You'd think so wouldn't you. You'd hope so.

Seemed something outside just now. Someone. I went to look but there wasn't. Phantoms, raccoons — "the possibilities are endless" (Spinoza? maybe or a wallpaper ad). Nothing on the tube again tonight (why I should think —). I got out the tapes I made in the winter February thereabouts. Remember I wrote you I'd tape the war? I did, or parts. Forgot though to label (how to label). Some of it any rate, the

abasia – inability to walk for which no physical cause may be found

abhorrence –

abjection – state of misery or degradation

abscess –

first fuzzy days — nights — a blue ghost circus over Baghdad. Hot today, 33 C, the air like sour mud in your throat, you wonder what compels you to inhale. Strange how this desert looks almost inviting. A "dry hot" (not to sound insane).

Paul suggested his analyst. He means well, that's clear, one he leaned on when he made his voyage through divorce (not suggesting) and I took down the name. Konrad. More to please Paul. I told him if the word maybe didn't start with "anal" — but Paul says my problem's with money, or so he said his analyst said when he heard about me balking at the rate, or not so much money as the claim of concern over money when what it is (or might be) is a way of masking my fear of confronting my problems by way of an otherwise wholly commendable frugality(!). I had to laugh. I mean I would've, had I someone to laugh with. Someone not being analyzed. (This is not a shot at Alice. I don't hate Alice. Whatever advice she gave you (?), whatever conclusions she "encouraged" you to draw — regarding us — is fine, and if it wasn't for that glimpse I had, that day I picked you up after the appointment, the two of you were leaving together — the building — were walking out — normal enough — and I thought who's that shrewd-looking woman with Muriel, "shrewd" was the word, she looks like a goddam rocket scientist or something — and then to discover the true nature of her work and

absorption – disappearance through incorporation in something else

abulia – absence or impairment of will power

acalculia – acquired inability to make simple mathematical calculations

accident(s) –

her name being Alice and why I thought rockets, and then — or later — who is this person, this CRITICAL INTELLIGENCE, showing up on our shared path, like a fork in the road, but leaning your way, in the sense that she never got my position, she never got the other side of the story (I know it's not a story, not like we're antagonists (strictly speaking) but it's intimate, what goes on between two people, the intimacy), and having this stranger (stranger named Alice) suddenly there, her ear to those things you probably find too intimate, too compromising to divulge to even me, there's something — I don't think it's over-reacting to say I somehow found it something of a threat. "Intrusive bitch" was not the best choice of words. I realize now she was only doing her job.

Watching the bombs (strange, in retrospect, no longer swept along in the frenzy), to watch the bombs fall — the bombs being ours. Our side's. To sit at home. Here a bus stop, here a barracks, here a palace, here a bridge. Douglas Fairbanks nowhere in sight. Neither is Sinbad. Neither are you. Into my eighth finger of Scotch (ogre's fist), bathed in blue, the monochrome, the whisper of missiles, guessing Bali. Kuala Lumpur? 12 hr difference. Afternoon. On some beach, some sacred site. Paul says hi. We spent the night in the faculty lounge, getting vague. I don't know if I believe in the brain. Said as much. Paul's assistant found this very witty, praised me no end. Wit

accouchement – delivery of a baby

acedia – laziness, torpor

acrodermatitis – inflammation of the skin of the feet or hands; can result finally in atrophy (see below) should be met — if at all — with wit. Nothing worse for wit than praise. I didn't say this. Perhaps I should've. And if he only knew the source.

Mood-swings continue, whether due the Ballantines (& aftermath), weeks w/o a letter, this being alone, or the ongoing strain of putting up with the stuffy stupefaction with which any of my summer session planning meeting motions are met. Try to not at least stink of the stuff when I pass through, which is less and less. Passed the Canterbury course to Paul. What it is about standing in front of a class these last few months I don't know. Had the thought of pissing my pants, in front of them, just for effect, to stand there speaking quite reasonably while the urine wandered its wide way down, to see how they'd react, if at all. And since the occurrence of this thought, I've lost a good bit of my concentration, it shifting instead to the sending of signals down to the bladder, the urethra, a firm but civil NO (tone is crucial). Managed an argument with Johnson today. It didn't take much. Concerning the war. You know that fierce clarity that comes sometimes? I went into the office (don't ask me why) this morning, four maybe five hours sleep, mental limping, my throat like dust. Paul wasn't in (proof of his wisdom), so I found myself alone at the coffee pot. Johnson came over for water for his herbal tea, perhaps that's why, what struck a chord. I was suddenly saying how the bombing of Iraq, of the Tigris and Euphrates, had less to do with oil and tyrants than with wiping out the cradle of the Western world. This, in conjunction with the plan to redirect water from the Rockies, from Hudson Bay, to the Mississippi and LA badlands, would clear the way for America to claim that the "true West" rose up on the shoulders of American enterprise and ingenuity, a new river system which would run up and down, north south east west, the length and breadth of the continent, its name (what else but) — the America. Johnson scowled. He's got dual citizenship. He asked for my sources. I told him, the Unconscious. This didn't sit well. He called (as always) my nationalism blinkered, over-earnest, daft, my anti-Americanism paranoid and fuelled by self-interest and transparently hurt feelings at being passed over for Assistant Head in favour of that dolt from Pittsburgh (which I partially acknowledge). I hastened though to add that we — the Canadians — would not be excluded, we would have our role: as dam-builders, local labour, local colour, planners, advisors, and architects of our own demise. What is it when stern pasty men in tweed sip herbal tea and watch your lips? The man's the same goddam age as me, but he makes me nervous (maybe the booze), he is not "above" me, he's merely this resolutely drab authori-

acrophobia – morbid dread of heights

Addison's disease – (no longer fatal)

aestivation – spending of summer (esp. Zool.) in state of torpor

affliction(s) –

agnosia – disorder whereby patient cannot interpret sensations correctly although sense organs and conductive nerves are functioning normally

agnosticism –

agony(s) – (general, specific)

tative thing that stands there, his own lips like two garden slugs making (if you'll excuse the term) love. I spewed all sorts of inanities — the list I'm making on what can go wrong, in the most basic sense, a catalogue of perils, conditions, distractions, that can stall/stun/cripple one over the course of the journey; why I want pencils, paper — all manner of recording devices — restricted from my classes; what he thought (it being his speciality) of *Beowulf's* Grendel being in fact a Sasquatch. The first two I might've gotten away with, but the third clearly struck a raw nerve. His lips separated, his grey teeth protruded, awash in camomile (meant to soothe). He turned away but in turning said something I didn't manage to quite make out. Fuck you in Anglo-Saxon is my guess. Never utter it in English of course. Too new. Less than half a millenium. Still the taste of useage upon it.

8 p.m., still at the office. Going through papers, thinning files, a kind of purge — unsure though yet of what. The bulk, the terminal accumulation, the things you think that maybe somewhere down the line ... Boxes and boxes and boxes and boxes. Very nearly forty minutes staring into one in particular. Nothing of interest. Just looking down. You see why the list. You think it's you — Muriel — who's travelling, who's gone away, is making tracks, consuming horizon

with such great abandon. But I'm the one who leaves as I sit, spiralling in darkness broken only by glimpses (too brief) of daylight and debilitating fits of cognition. I want the possible trajectories marked out, should it come that I have to "see" someone. Nice to know at least what's going. Gone. What seems now to never have been. Calm, equilibrium. Spoke with the janitor — George — mentioned the thing about Grendel. He liked the idea but thought I'd need bones. To make it fly. Of course he's right. He brought in some baklava. Asked my advice about a brilliant daughter. Rocket science I almost said. Analysis. But she's into the classics. I couldn't believe someone into the classics, that age, hers I mean, to be seventeen, to be thrilled by dead languages, somehow, anymore. I'm worrying now most about decorum. I almost want to take George's advice, walk in (where I'd get it I don't know) one day into Johnson's office, lay on his desk a three-foot-long petrified femur or tibia, say "Here's your Grendel" and leave. The wit is not the first to go. Hygiene maybe, nutrition, civility, but wit hangs around to the bitter end (perhaps not bitter, perhaps just ghastly — to me, one who's been paid by his brains, to have to come to terms with a mind unmoored, roaring on through dark, aware and incompetent, aware of just such incompetence — perhaps I'm biased, ghastly seems fit).

agoraphobia – morbid fear of public places, open spaces

agromania – pathologically strong impulse to live alone in open country

air embolism – air lock obstructing outflow of blood from right ventricle

akinesia – loss of normal muscular tonicity and responsiveness

Alphabet: alpha, beta — why on earth it should end at "z" —

Thought I saw you on the street today. It was not you (rest assured) but I had to get within several feet to search out the details which made it not so. This woman talks, dresses like you and, Muriel, I swear — height, weight, hair colour, nose — but the mouth is too broad, the hips a touch slimmer. I had to speed up, pass her, stop, and pretend to consider some over-priced oranges. She too was looking over fruit, looked up a moment, it was all I required. You know I thought she almost smiled, a sort of recognition, but it couldn't have been. I'd have noted the resemblance. I'd have — no. What the hell could there be to be gained — Hi you're the spitting image of my wife, I feel like I know you? No, I can't see it. (Thinking of the article Kay likes to quote, of all men being potential rapists due to the peninsula jutting from their groin (is this why I cannot talk to Kay?). Of course we are also potential saints, salesmen, and everything in between.) The thing is I did feel compelled to say some-thing, approach her, I did feel this terrible draw. To study her, hang on her every ges-ture, follow her home (I didn't — I wouldn't!), only — only to see almost you, from a dis-tance, before I knew you. To see you (i.e. — a version of you) as someone to whom I did not matter, could just as easily not exist. I

alarmism – often unwarranted exciting of fears, warning of dangers

alexia – acquired inability to read

algolagnia – sexual perversion in which pleasure is got from inflicting pain on oneself or others looked back and she was gone. I'd bruised a peach, so bought it.

Paul's book finally came out, *Blind in One I: Re-Approaching Narration*, and they had a small reception in the lounge. I arrived numb and things went from there. Paul misquoted himself at length, Palliser passed out, Lydia left with a boy at work on his first moustache, and Johnson and I again locked horns. I said it was time for a movie of *Beowulf*, Arnold Schwarzenegger as the Geat. (I honestly do believe he'd do fine, the muscles, the accent that no one could actually prove was not Geat — besides, he doesn't say much.) Johnson flinched, but rebounded quickly. He asked who I saw in the role of the monster. I'd barely opened my mouth when Paul said Chamberlain — "Wilt Chamberlain, in moss." Johnson didn't recognize the name. We had to tell him. Can you believe it? What's the joy in baiting a man who swallows the bait and carries on regardless? I lost all interest and drank too much. I slurred. Johnson made some snide comment. I missed it, I gathered from Paul it was snide. I confronted Johnson, asked him whether — as I had it — he'd been snide. He asked was there a law against being snide. He would clearly neither confirm nor deny if he'd been IT with regard to me. I raised my voice, it seems I gave him something in the way of a small shove, a little push-off of my

alidade – (lack of) instrument for determining direction

alienation – estrangement; a turning away or diversion *from*; (psych) 1 – experience that others participate in one's thinking; 2 – insanity

alimentation – (lack of) nutrition, maintenance

palm from his lapel. Werner intervened and asked why I was angry. I couldn't — you know — precisely express it. The thing is Johnson did not seek redress, he knew his part in it, he got his coat and left. Paul was obliged to make the rounds. I killed some time in a corner booth, looking professional, pissed and perplexed, and could've remained there comfortably had it not been for Werner's voice, thick and insistent, him holding court with three of his students several feet off. These three could well've been sisters, not so much by looks as by gritty allegiance. Werner must've recognized a challenge. He plunged right into his favourite reminiscence of masturbating in the shallows off Tahiti and watching the little fish gobble his sperm. For whatever reason the three of them stayed, listening it seemed — can it be that it works? The lumberjack muscles, the Kerouac-quote tattoo . . . Can it be that we're all so desperate for myth that we're willing to be blinded to

alluvion – 1 – . . . . 2 – flood

Alzheimer's – progressive dementia occurring in middle age

amaurosis – partial or complete blindness

amazement –

be fed? I know you've always thought Werner an asshole, but how do these assholes get so often laid? I know we said we'd leave ourselves open ("open" was the word?) — to what, I wonder now. I'm in a corner. You're on some brink. I'm sitting with a glass between me and the world. Or was. Six feet between me and this student, close enough, even just to speak, to offer a hand out of the vortex of Werner's ego — in exchange for my own? My glass was empty, I'd been watching the one who seemed least enthralled by Werner's self-advertisements. She was smoking and blowing the smoke out the side of her mouth with a kind of Popeye expression, and drinking Scotch or rye or something amber and straight enough it seemed to sting her tongue with every sip. She's taking notes, I told myself, she's standing there letting this asshole satirize himself — or satyrize (and probably would, could he bend the thing far enough around). She shifted and turned a quarter-face away from him, a third, a half, she was now as much in my sphere as his, and our eyes met, Werner's and mine, as our glances rode the wild terrain of that body decades younger than our own. Our eyes met and Werner winked, all the while keeping up the tale of his exploits, and I thought — you bastard — and made up my mind. I stood and as quickly sat back down. My glass in one hand, Paul's book in the other, I lacked a third to stuff in my pocket and redirect a sudden rising. The girl, oblivious to both of us, dropped the butt in the bottom of her glass, swished it about, the hiss more dismissive than any remark she might have made. She placed the dead drink on the mantel behind her, turned, and walked off and out of the room. Werner came to the end of his sentence, and one of the other two started in on Chatwin's study of Australian aborigines.

ambiguity –

ambivalence –

amblyopia – poor sight not due to any detectable disease of the visual system

Perhaps I've been misled by wit. Perhaps it *is* the devil's tool. Wit a weapon against faith. That there is no final joke to be gotten, for which we'd been grooming our wit all along. That the joke is on us, and not of the ha-ha variety, but sick. Sick in the extreme.

No mail today. Or the mailman came, brought coupons, flyers, unaware of the risk. I'd sat in the front room for 2 hrs 20, having awakened with the absolute knowledge that a letter from you would come today, knowing the earliest the mailman has come is 10 to 9 and I was there no later than a quarter to. Coffee, a head that's been brought up too quickly from ten thousand leagues below the sea. 2 hrs 25 mins later the mailman came and dropped off coupons. I waited till he walked from the door, till he was gone before I went to see. Going to see, I did not yet know there were only coupons, I knew he'd stopped, I'd heard the squeak and rattle and clump of the whole procedure. I felt somehow that if he'd seen me — before actually placing the letter in the box — if he'd caught a glimpse of my an-ticipation, my "need" for a letter, the "need" would pass from me to him, run down his arm, the selective acidity of the "need" being triggered by the discovery of the longed-for note, the letter would dissolve, the letter that may have been in his hand in the best of all possible worlds (which does not include par-allel worlds, the companion world to the one of the letter, the world which did not contain such a letter, not today, not perhaps ever). The thing then is that no letter came, I checked the other boxes, I checked the one next door, I stood on the walk and studied the path between the buildings, the path the mailman habitually takes. He was standing talking to a neighbour two doors down. He didn't see me, not at first. I thought to approach him — but what to say — seeing his answer would have to be that if there'd been a letter he'd have placed it in my box. The neighbour was saying something about his "wife as a rule" doing this or that. His wife as a rule. If that's what he believes. I laughed, as much for their benefit as mine. They must've recognized in the laugh more irony than humour, for they turned and stared. I nodded and they both nodded back. O little town of Bedlam, I said — softly, to myself.

Held off drinking (in spite of the above) tonight until 6, tomorrow 6:30, maybe 7, till gradually . . . Don't make me laugh, someone said on the streetcar today, several seats back. I didn't take it personally. To the best of my knowledge my thoughts have yet to actually start leaking from my skull.

The woman went by again today, the woman who looks like you. She was wearing something like harem pants, slippers with the toes curled up, a vest, blouse, this you will see — you will see the staggering — in her arms,

ambush –

amentia – failure of development of the intellectual faculties

ametropia – abnormality of refraction of the eye

amnesia –

amok (amuck) – sudden
outburst of furious and
murderous aggression,
directed indiscriminately
at everyone in the vicinity

amourette – petty love affair

amputation –

books, an armload of books, and dangling
from one hand a see-through net bag containing fruit. I watched in a sort of stunned
disbelief. I thought about that time in Van-
couver, 1981 remember, when I swore I saw
Lucky? Beckett's Lucky, Hemlock and 4th,
something and 4th. Hemlock, Yew, one of the
tree names. Trudging downhill, toward the
harbour. We'd gone out to get some acid for
the weekend (acid one could trust), the guy
didn't show, we didn't know that then, that
he wouldn't, we were very much in a state of
innocence. You stopped in a little store for
trail mix, I stood on the corner, I was facing
the harbour, and to my right, not five feet
away, Lucky appeared, pausing at the lights.
The pause went on through two complete
traffic light interchanges, he hardly seemed to
breathe. I thought, alright he breathes
through his pores. There were those around
then who'd made it a career. The traffic re-
sumed, which was when he veered out, right
into it, through it, like it wasn't there.
Everyone stopped, as much to stare as to stop
their vehicles from challenging him. He was
6'5", in a suit for an overweight businessman
of 5'9", with a bowler hat that had seen better
days (what bowler hasn't), a suitcase bound
with a belt and his pants secured to his hips
with a rope. His eyes were blue (a bird's I remember), the pupils barely pinholes, irises
you could swim in. Several days unshaven,
thin grey hair to just past the shoulders, nose

a wedge, mouth the scar of a wound long healed over. The breathing when it came was a wheeze, the smell a vaguely vegetable rot. Dingy white shirt w/o a collar, no socks, and laceless oxfords. It didn't take much to see who he was. You were still inside, delayed at the checkout, the clerk was trying to open the register with pliers. I stood there, caught between wanting to run after him, demand some speech, maybe rearrange his hat, that or haul you from the store, drag you along till you'd caught a glimpse. I didn't do either. I can't say I "regret" it. I stood transfixed. I thought blessed. My glance wavered back and forth between the two of you, you oblivious standing with your trail mix, Lucky now slipping in and out of the last sun breaking between the buildings. By the time you emerged, he of course was gone. You liked my story but that's all it was to you, a story about an uncanny resemblance. You managed to coax some mushrooms from Arnold, airport-field, later on when it became clear the acid-guy would not show. I passed on the mushrooms. You didn't understand. It's fixed in my mind, that struggle over meaning. I think you thought I was talking similarities. I don't think you truly grasped who it was I'd seen.

Last night again the measured tumble (glass by glass) into furniture land. Watched to the end of the bombing tape. Followed by commercial, deals on cars. Had on the VCR for the tape. I scanned the dial, happened on a

anabiosis – state of suspended animation induced by way of dessication

anachronism – person or thing out of harmony with time

anascara – swelling of legs, trunk, genitalia, due to fluid-retention

angina –

scrambled transmission of "I Dream of Genie" reruns. Put on "record" in spite of interference. Sporadic bolts jerking Genie back and forth across the screen, her perky good-nature, taut cream tummy. Managed to freeze-frame on her bending halfway over to offer fruit. Spit in one hand, a sock in the other, my cock lurching up through the alcohol — it seemed the shadow in the satin crotch got even more provocative a couple seconds further. My thumb banged about (spastic with spit), fast-forward to rewind to slow to freeze, again and again but it only got worse. When finally I let the fiasco cease, the image was Genie nearly erect, her arms as if paralyzed at her sides, her throat a grotesquely brilliant blur, the chest collapsed, the waist disrupted in a cross-screen slash of wicked light. My cock shrank, a tiny bauble of come at the tip the only suggestion of what had gone before. I fell asleep in the chair, and into fitful dreams, one in particular of being caught in a storm at sea. I get a hold of the *Moby Dick* coffin — Queequeg's — but so it happens does Grendel. I'm thinking what if he tries to drown me, he has that look — but then there's commotion. Lucky and Frankenstein's monster surface on the other side, struggling for handholds. We come to an agreement, we take a handle each. The sea calms as we talk. Frankenstein's monster has an F sewn on the front of his jersey, so we call him that. He's shy, sensitive, pretty well-spoken. A bit green, but then we all are.

angst –

anguish –

(annihilation –)

anosmia – loss of the sense of smell

Grendel's hairy, but otherwise civil, and Lucky's as he was on the street. We all come from different walks of life, but all feel peripheral, so have that in common. Soon an island appears nearby. On it is a woman sitting in a sundress. She has a bottle of wine beside her. Has on sunglasses but I'm pretty sure it's you. She waves. I don't know whether to wave back, lead them ashore, in view of reputations. They tell me I can go alone. It's unclear though what might be in the water. I hesitate. It becomes a beach. Crowded. You get up and wander off. I check and find the water's only up to our knees. The others go swimming. They're magnificent swimmers. I open the coffin, which is now a trunk. In it are my papers, soggy and ruined.

Perhaps you realise I don't expect you back. Or would — you would, should you come upon this. As for the woman, was she a woman (on the street) — or was she a sign? The books — whose books? The fruit — indigenous to nowhere at all? Had I a telescope, had I more of that which does not come from books. FEAR RULES it said on some construction site wall I passed last night, so what is one to do? Make a point of confronting Fear, to let it not lead us into spinelessness? In every dog prepare to see Cerberus, hold all "development" up against the suffering of F, of Lucky and Grendel? It's just after 4 a.m. — again — the palace is quiet. Knowing some things, the TEMPORALITY of things, the thing of

antinomy – paradox

aphasia – disorder of language affecting speech, its understanding

aphrenia – failure of development of the intellectual faculties

apnea – temporary cessation of breathing

knowing nothing, of knowing merely that. This thing of thinking, when I look on this later and it no longer means, of words not meaning — a thing, that I may well wake tomorrow and not know these words, or what words are. For now, maybe that I am merely me, and my name's Tom (or thereabouts), knowing full well one can't live forever, are finally finally left for dead, through no preventable "fault" of one's own, this Tom for instance this tom this man figure standing in the mirror, this tom named me attempting to somehow prepare to meet its god —

TOM / GOD

TMO / GDO

OTM / ODG

OMT / OGD

MTO / DGO

MOT / DOG

Out the window the rain is falling — or more like something that has lost its way, is drifting down, a dense confused exodus from the sky, density increasing as it nears the ground. Streetcars gently press their way through, the odd cab, now & then a figure —

Two things that should perhaps be said — by way of background, significance: 1. Growing up, the most traumatic experience I daily endured was on my early-morning paper route. One of the customers kept three black dogs, large, loud and aggressive (those were not

apoplexy – (see stroke)

apostasy – abandonment of faith, vows, principle, party

apparition –

apraxia – inability to make skilled movements with accuracy their names). She kept them inside ("as a rule"), but the mail slot was several inches from the ground, through which the paper was to be put, to the left of the door and directly below a sheet of plate glass 1' wide and 7' maybe 8' high. I'd almost always make it to the door without the dogs hearing, I would have the paper halfway through, when suddenly — always suddenly — out of the dim recesses of the corridor first one then the other then the other would appear. The width of the window made it such that no more than one of them could hit the glass at the same moment — so they'd rotate. The image was that of one huge body with three heads, all of which seemed solely bent on tearing mine from me. Our faces a foot and a half apart, separated by 3/4" glass. 2. My favourite story at that time was H. G. Wells's "The Door in the Wall," in which a man out strolling discovers, quite by accident, a door which leads to Paradise. But it's temporary, his visit is brief, and his life from then on is spent in preoccupation with the door. His life, from one point of view, is RUINED by this first vision which haunts him thereafter. The ending is, in the best sense, ambiguous.

The "figure" I saw from the window last night (or morning — however you care to view these things) seemed to be none other than the woman I'd described. She raised her hand — I thought at first a wave — to me — but in fact she was hailing a cab. I grabbed my

aprosexia – inability to fix attention on a subject

arachnidism – poisoning from the bite of a spider

arrest –

arthritis –

asininity –

asphixia –

(assassination –)

astasia – inability to stand for which no physical cause may be found

coat and ran downstairs. Another cab was along shortly and the taillights of the first could still be made out through the thickening mist at the bottom of the street. We followed it as best we could. I described her to the cabbie as a friend who was leaving that day and had left with me by accident something quite essential. The driver asked if I didn't have the address. I said no, unfortunately. Friend of yours? he said with a tone. I said some people like to cultivate the mysterious, that it's no reflection on their integrity. He said, whatever, so long as I was flush. I placed a folded twenty on the dashboard and little else was said between us as we drove. Once or twice she seemed to elude us, but soon enough the taillights reappeared. He said he couldn't be sure it was her. I told him be strong and of good courage (after which he said even less). I suddenly made out where we were — a street adjacent to the old Necropolis. The lights on the cab ahead brightened with braking. I said to keep a distance. He didn't like that. He said maybe I should get out there, stopped, made change, a few dollars back, with little or no expectation of a tip. I said here's a loonie. He said "no guff." I hadn't heard the expression in years. I got out. He drove off without another word. The other car was still parked some ways ahead. The cab I'd been in, it pulled up alongside, there was some sort of interchange, then they both drove off. I saw what looked like the figure moving along the sidewalk on the street perpendicular to the one on which I stood. The pace was brisk. I wouldn't catch up without running, and thereby drawing attention. However, if I scaled the fence, took a shortcut through the Necropolis — which is what I did. Getting over was simple enough, snagged a trouser cuff on one of the iron pales but with a tug it was free, and once beyond the pales (as it's said) . . . The place was quiet, as one might expect. I paused and took a flask from my pocket, took a sip, just in case. I tried to make out the moving figure beyond the fence, beyond the fixed figures, the latter of which were, of course, abundant. The mist made a mess of depth of field, trying to gauge approximate distances. I started to move at a 45 degree angle from the fence, which should have sufficed. But once the fence was lost from view this became next to impossible. I neared a bench. Turning to sit, I came face to face with the cemetery dog. How long he'd been there, trailing me (minutes? years?), I'd no way of knowing. All the times you've felt breath on your neck, assumed a draft, and did not turn. Here boy, I said. Extended my hand. But he stayed put, a couple yards off. I pulled up my legs beneath me on the bench. Only the mist continued to move, in waves, veils, slow flocks of light. Birds began, which usually awakens me. Usually I'd shut the window at this time. Instead, I felt drowsy, I was in the prone position. Why I say "he." Why I

asthenia – weakness or loss of strength

asthma –

asyndesis – disorder of thought in which normal associations of idea are disrupted say "boy." I've truly no idea what the dog's gender was.

Security located me just about dawn. Intact, untouched, the dog gone. After a brief chat with the guard he took down my name but said they'd waive charges on the grounds my trespassing appeared to lack "intent." Suggested I not be found there again between the hours of dusk and dawn. Suggested I maybe have a chat with my doctor. I mentioned Bergman's *Hour of the Wolf*. He regretted not knowing it, knew only *Cries and Whispers, The Seventh Seal, The Passion of Anna*. We talked and talked. I was giddy with rapport, something, finding a common tongue. I would've been happy to stay there longer, but he had his report, the mists were lifting, the people blind with daylight were rising. I forgot to even mention the dog, to compliment them on the excellent training, until I was already halfway home. The streetcar slowed in the rush-hour traffic, I decided to why not stroll the remainder. It took a little over an hour and a half, by which time the mail had come, including (of course) your postcard from Nepal. Four weeks' time — I can hardly believe it! Under a month before we again — to just say *we*, to again be *able*! I checked my limbs for puncture wounds. How in the world can I feel this good? This week I start preparation for my fall course, "The Monster in Literature." I'm very excited. I shall make a categorical apology to Johnson.

ataxia – shaky movements, unsteady gait due to brain's failure to regulate posture and direction of limbs

atony – state in which the muscles are floppy

atrophy – (even worse)

My shins in fact look cooked in milk. I need sun. Can it be that simple? It's nine in the evening and I've yet to have a drink. The bottle lurks, I know it's there, but I'm holding off. Holding off. 9:30 showing is Murnau's *Nosferatu*. The first b-word of any application is "bacillemia," the presence of bacilli in the blood. Be that as it may, one persists. I think of the dams we built in Nepal, the bombs we escorted down upon Baghdad.

Here I sit with a garlic sandwich. You probably think I'm kidding. I am not kidding. The garlic, of all things, thrived this year. I will claw my way back to flesh and blood. I was human once. I'm certain.

authorisation – (lack of)

autointoxication – poisoning by a toxin formed within the body

automobility – (lack of)

awe –

OMENS

Saying I'm a sensitive person, I don't say that to brag. I taped this list of things that cause depression, things to watch out for, onto the fridge: cholesterol, coffee, excess protein, lack of exercise, high fat intake, alcohol, smoking, emotional stress, excess sugar, excess salt. Smokes I been off for seventeen months (and counting), I eat okay, I swim and bike, and booze I'm almost sensible with. Where I let slip was emotional stress. And it wasn't even my own.

Gwen says you can't save other people's lives. She's a nurse. She means in the general sense. She's seen some things — chronic behaviour, donut fiends with heart conditions, those who come in dying of their spouses, or exhausted from the grief of others. She says she waits for miracles, personally and professionally, not that she expects them. I couldn't. You might as well wait for evolution. Me, I pretty much have to numb out the part of the brain that makes me aware on a day-to-day basis, how people operate. Some of the chemicals I work with help. Still you can wind up open to stuff, other people's stuff coming in the back door.

Darlene drops by one day, this is months ago, just for a visit, she says at the start. It's mid-afternoon so I offer her a beer, it doesn't seem stupid, ones my boyfriend Lloyd left, European something or other — *Tuborg* maybe or *Heineken*. Anyhow Darlene says sure and drinks one, puts it back like water, which should've been a sign. She makes some comment how beer is beer and where do the Europeans get off thinking theirs is so superior. Then she has another.

Three have gone down and she's into her fourth before I can get near what she wants. I work restoring furniture and mostly I work at home and my work-space I like 'cause it gets for one thing so much light. Afternoons are the best time. I can live with disruptions, it's not that, but it's not like Darlene's a close friend, or that I asked her to drop by whenever. We met at a party, what kept us in contact was her needing a sitter on occasion. Simon's eight but might as well be fifty. The father's one of those guys who calls up every couple months to apologize. He can't make support, his money's tied up in a scheme that's always about to take off, after which of course there'll be piles, trips to Jamaica, bicycles. Simon's got a bike, one he bought himself from money he made selling chocolate bars. He listens to the promises, he knows them well. So does Darlene, but she still half-believes them. Simon says his Dad likes to talk, that's how he puts it — likes to talk. That's all he says. It's enough.

Comes out it wasn't so simple as a visit. Darlene's dying of cancer, she tells me, businesslike, through this mouthful of smoke. I nearly fall right off my chair. But Darlene wasn't looking for sympathy, what she needed to know was whether or not I'd consider adopting Simon. She said she probably had half a year anyway, but this wasn't something you could put aside. I asked about Carl, her ex, or any other relative or friend of the family.

"I thought *we* were friends," she goes.

I tell her we are. Meaning as opposed to enemies.

She launches into the whole long mess of her childhood, the neglect and gunshots and so on. She says she'd as soon not have any of them know. And it all came back, the first

night we talked, at that party, how I couldn't believe someone could chat about that shit so calmly, especially with a
stranger. I thought about how protected I'd been, having a
family that hugged and talked. I'd had some hairy times myself, but stuff more often than not I'd had a hand in, getting
too high in the wrong circumstances, not knowing the language in a scary foreign bar.

Daryl at this point she hadn't known that long, she'd
opened her legs but not a lot else. I just figured it was on-
again-off-again, that even she wasn't sure there was anything
to count on behind the strut and asshole facade. What I need
actually's an early warning system, some kind of radar, or filter
attachment I could strap to my head, it's ridiculous. Without
much thought — I'd had some beers myself — I look around
the kitchen and tell her sure, I'd be there for Simon, I
wouldn't let her down. She tells me not to worry myself,
who knows, a cure might be just around the corner, or
maybe she'd find a way to fight the thing off. I thought, holy
shit, this woman's made of steel, I asked her what kind of
cancer it was but she changed the topic, and I figured — fine.

It's none of my business what Darlene sees in Daryl, besides
the fact that their names sound close. Maybe his authority,
how he's got an answer to every question, he answers things
that aren't even questions, and on the rare occasion he *asks*
one you know you've only got so many seconds before he
goes and answers it himself. So whenever he'd say things like
how you doing I'd shrug and let him fill in the blank. I have
my dark days, ones you could sit and watch the house burn
down around you, drink a glass of Varsol, but you don't,
something stops you. I sure wasn't going to bring this up
with Daryl. So, instead, he brings up Lloyd.

Lloyd's a photographer, the kind that travels. We met
through the Skills Exchange, we shared a classroom. He's not

ambitious but he makes a living. Me too, when it comes to that. The big surprise was he wasn't a control freak. I actually lost it to a photographer, I was seventeen, he was twenty-eight. He liked to call me *water nymph*, took all these pictures of me in the bath. My skin'd pucker, but he said be patient, he'd learned when you dealt with the photo muse the central thing was patience. I'm average-looking, I got no delusions. But when you're seventeen, and getting called a water nymph, you can end up in bathtubs way more than you need. Lloyd believes in the photo muse as much as I do in the furniture muse. When I found out that, I knew we'd get along.

First time they met — Daryl and Lloyd — Lloyd was about to head off north to where all those caribou got wiped out. Another similar wipe-out was expected, courtesy the power dams. Daryl asked Lloyd if he'd lived in the North. When Lloyd said no, Daryl said maybe then he wouldn't fully understand the job creation aspect. Lloyd sort of lied. He was born in the Yukon, but his parents moved south when he was two. Daryl was born in Parry Sound, a couple hours north of Toronto, and anyone who does not know this has not listened. Their conversation went downhill from there, the next time they met they hardly spoke, but Daryl continued to ask me how he was. I didn't lie, I let him know. Lloyd had opportunities coming out his ears. Most recently, south, stuff on peasant communities surviving without the CIA.

Daryl had come by to pick up Darlene, which was just as well since the beers were gone, and I dreaded getting sober in that room with her then.

"So he just takes pictures?" Daryl wants to know.

I toss out an estimate for sales for the year.

"Lucky guy," he goes. "Some of us work."

Daryl's work is renovating houses. It'd been pretty tough of course with the recession, but he made a bundle during the boom. Darlene told me once, in strictest confidence, he had this idea of being an architect but couldn't take the thought of going back to school.

"Work's what pay's the bills," I go, and notice my hands which are a sight in themselves. I'd gouged a knuckle a couple days before, and run out of mineral spirits halfway through a bitch stain job on an antique chair.

"Nicky," goes Daryl, "what we do's work." Meaning not wimp-shit, meaning me and him. Whenever we meet he wants to test my grip. I got some pretty big staple guns. But picture-taking he figures is fun, or else people wouldn't do it on their holidays. He's got a camera himself, a new one, and all you got to do so he says is point the thing in the right direction. Camera does the rest. I don't argue.

This is maybe two months later, and with Darlene I'd walked a fine line. I didn't mean to, it just sort of happened, she didn't broach the issue and neither did I.

I'm bringing Simon back after having him one Saturday. It's late afternoon, a nice spring day, and we'd been to the park and thrown a basketball around. I used to play a lot really, got scouted by some schools in the States, but never got my act in gear to end up actually going.

Daryl had moved in a few weeks before and his presence was everywhere, inside and out. He had this sixty-something Chevy he'd dug up out of a Springsteen song spread out in pieces across the backyard. He'd gone out looking, but all he found was one in perfect working order, which he'd had to then dismantle in order to build back up from scratch. Which was fine with Darlene. It kept him busy.

He looks up from a fender as we're coming in, and scowls. "Whose is that?"

"Mine," I go.

"Yours?" he goes. "What d'you need a basketball?"

"To play," I tell him.

Simon giggles.

"You shoulda told me," Daryl says to Simon. "You wanna play B-ball, I'll take you out."

Simon reminds him they don't own a ball.

"You want a ball, we'll get a ball," says Daryl, like a Dad.

Simon looks at me, then shrugs. Then follows me inside.

We're sitting on the couch, Darlene and me, we're having a beer, she's got on music videos, Simon's in the bath, and Daryl's still outside. It hits me — before she gets too wrecked — now might be a good time to talk. I ask how things are going, but vague-like, giving her the option.

"Okay," she says, like I asked about the weather. The video she's staring at isn't that exciting.

"Really?" I go, since *okay* doesn't say much.

She turns to look at me, her face is a mask. Then for some reason she breaks out laughing. Then she stops.

"Yeah," she goes, "Why?"

I start to think it's medication.

"You know," I say. "With the cancer . . . ?"

It's like I'm speaking in another language. Her face clouds over, she looks real puzzled, then it brightens like everything's fine.

"Oh . . . *that*," she finally goes.

Daryl marches in with a six-pack on a collar and takes a seat across from us. "I guess you might not realize," he says, "I used to play some ball myself."

I nod and turn right back to Darlene, but she's in the meantime gone spaniel over Daryl.

142

He asks if I ever heard what happened in the pen.

"Tell her, tell her!" says Darlene like it's Christmas.

"Easy, honey, the clock ain't runnin'," Daryl says with this cool grin. Not that I cared, but this was his story: he'd played in a league in Kingston in the seventies. They played other city teams, the colleges, and prisons. He couldn't remember which pen it was, but halfway through the game he caught an elbow from a convict, and waited till the ball came back his way. When it did, the guy was on him, Daryl turned, faked the shot, then swung the ball with all he had in a hard tight hook at the other's gut. Knocked his wind out. The guy dropped. The refs didn't see it, or if they did they must've thought it was a pass, they didn't call it. The main thing to Daryl was the convict *knew*. Daryl knew, and his buddies knew and the other team knew, even the spectators: no one screws with Daryl and walks away.

He throws back his head, and with it half a can of beer, shifts back forward, and looks at me.

I look at the TV but there's a commercial. I see Darlene's cigarettes right within reach, have to remind myself I don't smoke, I don't need that number for the trained professionals waiting on-call to talk me off the nicotine, it isn't the nicotine, what it is is needing something to shut my mouth.

"Sorry if I bored you," says Daryl.

"No," I say, "but it sounds pretty stupid."

Cut his throat the blood couldn't drain any faster from his face.

"It wasn't his fault," Darlene lets me know. "You gotta pay 'em back or they'll make you their doormat."

"Darlene," says Daryl. And that's all he has to. It's like he pulled her plug. He gets up, takes his beer and walks it around the room. "Some people," Daryl announces, "think they got the line on it all. They got a boyfriend who travels all over, who takes pretty pictures and sends them post-cards."

Lloyd, whether or not Daryl knew it, was down in Nica-ragua at that moment. There *had* been postcards and they had me worried. Lloyd was overwhelmed by the place and was looking into getting a placement. Which was all fine and good, except I don't speak Spanish, and redone Victorian somehow I doubt's a priority there. Least of all did I need Daryl's input.

"Ever wonder," Daryl goes, "what he's always doing on the other side of the world? Staying home nights writing you letters? Yeah, right, and I'm the Man from Glad."

I ask him (not very nicely) what his problem is.

He just smirks, turns and leaves.

Darlene shrugs, rolls her eyes, and smokes like no tomor-row. She won't defend him but she isn't going to criticize. Bloom's still on the rose, as they say.

"Honey, show her the tickets," Daryl yells in from the other room.

Darlene picks up her purse from the floor, and takes out an airline ticket envelope. She looks up from under her lids like they're curtains, says in this voice that's just learned how to talk — "Daryl's taking me on vacation. Club Med. The one in the Bahamas." Far as I knew they shared expenses. Meaning, I guess, it was his idea.

"Great," I say, like I'm taking a pill.

They had reservations for a few weeks away, they were waiting on their tax returns. The thing was, could I take Simon for the week? I tell her it's not a good time for me. Lloyd I was expecting back the very same weekend they were planning to leave.

"So you can't help me out," she says in this monotone.

"It's just me and Lloyd need some time," I say.

"Don't beg, Darlene." Daryl in the doorway. "We'll find someone else. I can think of ten people." But the names weren't charging to the tip of his tongue.

"Yeah," goes Darlene, and turns to the TV like I've ceased to exist.

I'm packing my stuff up when Daryl comes over and picks up the basketball.

"Y'mind?" I say. There's grease on his hands.

"Simon says you're pretty good," Daryl says, challenge dripping.

I shrug. I won't deny it. Not then. Not to him.

He goes to me, "How 'bout we have a little game?"

I tell him no, and reach for the ball.

"How come?" he says. "Think you're too good?"

I look at the floor and wait for him to finish.

"*Daryl . . .* " goes Darlene in this coaxy whine.

"Think fast!" Daryl shouts, throwing out his hands.

I catch the movement from the corner of my eye, a pass coming at my head, and I duck. It's that old trick where you let the ball drop but thrust out your hands like you're passing it hard. The ball hits the floor and he grabs it on the bounce. He's laughing with his teeth closed, which makes the air go out his nose in loud little gusts.

"Darlene," I say and turn to her, "can you train this asshole?"

"Think fast!" I hear again, just before the ball hits my face.

I can't say for sure that I'd actually kill Daryl, if circumstances presented themselves, but I sure can't say I'd prevent someone else. The throw wasn't as hard as it could've been — Daryl kept reminding us — accidents happen and this was one, his hands were greasy and the ball was worn, you couldn't grip it like you should be able to. I'm sitting in a chair and they're feeding me rye, not that I need it, but they're trying to be good hosts. Sitting there not even reaching up to touch it, I can feel the tissue swelling with blood above the eye. Darlene sends Daryl to the kitchen for ice, and there's actually an edge to her voice. He goes gets the ice and a cloth, brings me it, he's washed his hands, he's on his best behaviour, he's even wiped the ball off on his shirt. Simon comes in and asks what happened. Darlene tells him Nicky and Daryl were playing and Daryl threw the ball too hard. Daryl says nothing. I don't challenge her version. Simon's not stupid, he's known her eight years. Daryl offers me a ride home and when I tell him thanks but no thanks he looks like he could kiss my feet.

That night I'm on the phone with Gwen and it comes up me seeing Darlene.

"So . . . " goes Gwen, "she a skeleton yet?"

I don't know what to say for a sec. I ask her what she means.

Gwen's surprised, she thought I knew, she thought she told me weeks back how when she'd dropped in on Joan, this friend of ours, Darlene was there and, when Gwen came in, Darlene didn't get a chance to take Joan aside and tell her the cancer stuff was secret, to not say anything to Gwen, who — public knowledge — likes to talk. So anyhow Joan decides to get Gwen's input, seeing how Gwen works as a nurse, she might have ideas on what to do, where to go for support and so on. Gwen, instead, goes at the symptoms.

Gwen (whether or not Joan knew) had had cysts removed from her ovaries a while back. She'd gone the whole route of fear and speculation, not knowing how much to tell the kids, to tell anyone, afraid of pity, afraid of not knowing *how* to live whatever time she might have left, she only worked Emergency, she'd steered well clear of the units where people die gradually. Anyhow it seems they got it — the cancer — and Gwen came out the other end scarred, stunned, but in one piece. Still, she wasn't keen on the word.

It comes out Darlene's had not been confirmed, not entirely, not in fact at all. Darlene had read about changes in moles, that changes in moles were omens of cancer. Gwen asked her then and there to show them the moles. Darlene hesitated, she had good reason. Whether or not they'd done any changing, they weren't moles but *cherry angiomas*, little raised red spots that come and go, according to Gwen about as ominous as feet. Darlene claimed she'd never noticed them before, at least not that big. Not that red. Gwen let her have it. Darlene played the innocent, something Gwen says she's willing to buy in four out of five people under age ten. Darlene left in tears and a huff.

"Good riddance," says Gwen. "Good riddance from our lives." Then she must've remembered that I was still in contact, still having dealings. She changed the subject, it took us both some effort, like an itch you know you shouldn't claw.

The next morning a card comes from Lloyd saying he's going to be back two weeks early, which still left a while for the bruise to fade. Not that it had to, just that I thought it better if the whole thing with Daryl didn't have to come up. Also — and maybe it didn't make sense — I didn't want to walk down the street with people looking from my eye to Lloyd. Anyone who knows me or him wouldn't think that, I'd hope not anyway, that he'd do it, that he'd do it and I'd stick around. Still, I was thinking of some big sunglasses.

The phone rings and I turn off the bath, and I answer it and it's Darlene. She wants to know how my eye's doing, if there's much of a bruise.

"Yeah," I tell her, "we got some colour happening."

We chat a bit. There's not a lot to say. She does her best to apologize, without actually coming out and blaming Daryl. Half the blame she takes on herself, the rest she makes over like an Act of God, like a tornado hit me in the face. I'm feeling sorry for her, caught like she is, and once more my mouth gets ahead of my brain.

"I got a thing from Lloyd," I say. "He's coming back earlier, so if you still need someone to keep an eye on Simon . . ."

Darlene sighs and I bite my tongue.

"I *wish* . . . " she goes, "I'd *known*."

"I didn't know myself till today," I tell her.

"Well," she says, "we've made other plans. He's going to stay with Daryl's folks."

I ask does he know them?

She says no, but he might as well start. "Least they're willing," she adds. "I asked Joan too but you can guess her answer."

"I'm sure she had her reasons," I say. A bit too sure. The woman's not *stupid*.

"Yeah? Like talking to Gwen?" snaps Darlene.

"Gwen?" I go, like I've never heard the name.

"You haven't talked?"

"Sure."

There's a silence.

"It *could've* been cancer. We're not all experts, okay?" says Darlene. Her voice is a rasp, like she's slowly swallowing a lit cigarette.

"It's serious stuff . . . is all," I tell her, "what I think Gwen meant."

"I can't trust anyone. Why I bother . . . " she ends with a sigh. Nails on a chalkboard.

"I got a bath running, just a sec," I say.

I put down the phone and wait about a minute. Maybe two. There's no clock in sight. When I pick it up, she's still there.

"Daryl I can trust . . . but he's *it*," she says.

"Darlene," I go, "have you *talked* to someone?"

I know what I mean but I don't know if she does, till she hangs up, then it's clear. I unplug the phone, get in the bath, and it doesn't take long, soon I'm starting to feel a big weight slipping from my shoulders. Except for Simon, the fact of Simon living with that stuff every day. I plug the phone in and call her back. The machine is on, I might've guessed, Darlene there waiting to screen my apology, let me talk myself into a stupor, which I've done in the past — don't ask me why — trying to be a friend. But what I say, after the tone, is I've got no more room in my life for her shit, I specify *shit*, hoping she'll distinguish that from all else that makes up a person, there are places to take your shit these days, they cost, but maybe Daryl can throw in. I add I'll take Simon any time, I'll do what I can, he's a wonderful kid. The tape runs out as I'm concluding, but that's fine, I'd said my bit.

The thing I guess I mean is it's a step. If you want to reduce stress you sometimes have to take semi-drastic measures. I sink in the bath. I think of a plane crash, Daryl and Darlene going down in the ocean. With open mouths. It's a thought. It's not like I've got them there floating in pieces. They're just there, way the hell out, waving maybe, reviewing their lives. Darlene loves Simon and he probably loves her back — that'd be the problem, it's not fair to him. Daryl I could give two shits, but Darlene — I'm not so fed up I'd want her dead. I give them the sense to close their mouths, stick life preservers around their necks. Just in case. Erase the sharks.

Stuff happens. I've seen it before. Like, how would I feel if something did? The water, I make sure to make it warm, the tropics, it's actually like a Jacuzzi. Jacuzzi with miles on every side.

I could've made it the Arctic.

VACUUMS ■
■
■
■

And in thy seed shall all the nations of the earth be blessed; because thou hast obeyed my voice. (Genesis 22:18)

My two-year-old son is curled in my arms. Three a.m. he woke with *night terrors*. We are in a chair in the living room, the two of us rocking, him back to sleep and me toward those dreams we label memory.

I lived for a while in a small town in the mountains. No one especially wanted me there. I'd been wandering east when I ran into winter, so took a room — by chance — above the hardware store. Hardware stores engender hope. They are the churches of the mundane man. One can't roam the aisles of a hardware store without being overcome by The Possible. Which was just as well. The mines were laying off, and work of any sort was scarce. Ashtray of a town, it burned to the ground several times in its history. In my few months there, one barn went up in flames, two cars, three cats.

I was near the cash in the store one morning, describing the grim job search I was involved in — hitching fifteen miles out of town, in twenty below, to a truck-stop junction where someone sought a Japanese interpreter for wildlife tours. He'd yet to get the scheme off the ground, but took down my number, promising to call. I was distinct from the other applicants in that I spoke some Japanese.

Carl, at the register, mentioned I might try a fellow who had a janitorial firm. "Hans . . . ."

Another man broke in — "Enzyme."

Carl handed me a card, which I took — Hans Anheim, Janitorial Expert — more to seem interested in any kind of work than having particular interest in this. "He's through here most mornings. Just after eight."

"Watch yourself," a third man said.

"Specially on inclines," added the second.

The two men eyed me and I looked to Carl, who looked at his hands as though he'd just noticed them.

The sun rose twice those early winter mornings. It would break between the lower peaks, blaze briefly then angle into the ridge rising toward the highest mountain. Twenty minutes later, it would break from the mountain's other side and run its span till mid-afternoon when it slipped beyond the rock for good.

Between the two rises I would glance at the paper. The help-wanted column was three to four inches. I had twenty minutes, between the two rises, to find myself a place in that column. Twenty minutes to bang my head on the door of night, knowing it would not reopen for another eight hours, eight pale hours spent in wresting clear my idle hands from the devil. Usually the ads were seeking specialists, five to twenty-five years experience, degrees — none of them in Philosophy.

I did not call Hans, I ran into him. I was looking for bags for a vacuum the landlord had lent me to clear away generations of flies from between the windows. Two of the windows had been painted shut, and their outer storms on some years. The dirt-filtered light which struggled through made the days seem darker than they already were. I'd knifed the windows open, then found the flies.

Carl was giving me directions when Hans came in, and we were introduced.

Hans's face gave little as he spoke, even less when anyone else did. Carl made a gesture to the side of the head, and I noticed the wire snaking out of Hans's ear. I raised my voice. "You're looking for help?"

"Who told you that?"

I nodded to Carl.

"Help comes, it comes."

"I'm looking for work."

"What's to look for? Work is all around."

I looked at Carl, but Carl looked down. Rent was due in two weeks' time, and he could be witness to my initiative.

"I'm willing."

"Experience?"

"Cleaning?"

"Cleaning."

"He just come in for some vacuum bags," Carl threw in, to my defence.

"What's your equipment?"

"Hoover," I said.

Hans's jaw wandered around a bit.

"Got some in my truck. Prob'ly do the trick. Might have to improvise."

"What about the work?"

"If you want to work . . . if you *want* to work . . . be out front the store tonight at ten."

That night, at ten on the nose, the van pulled up and I got in. It took some doing. The sliding side door behind the passenger's popped free like a dislocated limb, then rolled back with a well-greased groan, exposing the tangled guts of the business. A power buffer, swinging about on its rotating head, hit a drum of floor-wax, which in turn capsized against a mop-and-bucket unit, propelling the latter into my unexpectant and, luckily, uncommitted hands. Once I was in it — the space allotted — nothing else fell, there was give-and-take, but the easy lurching of *things in place*.

I hadn't expected another worker, the quiet block of woman in the passenger seat. We drove a ways before Hans ran up on the need to speak.

"Keys?" His question was answered with a nod. We drove another minute in silence, then stopped in front of a bank.

"My wife of twenty-three years," said Hans.

For a moment I thought he meant the bank.

"Greta," said the woman, offering her hand, thick but immaculately clean and smelling strongly of scented soap.

Reaching from my cramped position, I briefly lost balance, and was steadied by her grip. Hans glanced over. Then, as quickly, away.

The work went easily enough. Hans, for all his brusque manner, dawdled. Greta gave what directions were needed, monitored the pace, and did her share. Hans would be carving down a fingertip callus with a penknife when Greta would gently inform him that it was time to leave. Once I noticed him swishing wax in a figure eight — two minutes straight on the same spot — I coughed, and he moved. Vacuuming, he seemed intent, but vacuuming was only a quarter of the work. The vacuum cleaner was the biggest I'd seen, three feet high, about a hundred pounds, with a fifteen-foot hose like an anaconda. It roared. And I thought about his hearing

— the loss — and whether the years of nights with that contraption were responsible.

At lunch Greta asked me my denomination. I understood the word, I just didn't use it. "Optimist," I managed, between bites.

"She means . . . ," Hans started.

"He can speak for himself." She paused, and appeared to ponder my response. "It's nice to hear other perspectives sometimes."

I nodded, and promptly broke eye contact, balled up the paper bag from my lunch and foul-shot it into the garbage can. We were in a car dealership. Cars do little for me. I got up and wandered over to the sleekest, shiniest one in the room, and studied it. A moment later Hans was at my side.

"She means your belief."

"This baby," I smirked, nodding to the crimson coupe.

Hans's face hardened, turning away.

"*Presbyterian.*" The word left my mouth as it had not in almost twenty years, not since I'd been confronted in a schoolyard where Jews and Catholics were being cursed. The word had carried surprising power, so many syllables off a small tongue, and the general confusion over what it meant. "Like *United*," someone had said, "only meaner," after which I was safe.

It stopped Hans. He looked me up and down, then threw a glance back to Greta. She put her things away, then washed her hands. Hans bent my way, his lips barely open: "Be needing it then — the optimism."

The roar of the vacuum precluded any rebuttal I might have wanted to make, were I still a Presbyterian. Had I, in fact, *ever* been, of my own volition. As things stood, I was happy just to bask in the din of our misunderstanding.

Hans dropped Greta off at their house as the sky in the

south-east was starting to brighten. He offered me the passenger seat, which I took, so as not to offend him. Since my declaration of "belief," Greta had been polite but distant, Hans seemingly preoccupied.

We neared the corner to the hardware store, but Hans didn't turn, he only pulled over to the curb, the street before us rising steadily toward the mountains. "Greta's happy with your work."

This surprised me. I couldn't think when they would've had a chance to discuss it. "Good," I muttered, the tone all wrong, as though saying — good for her. I'd just meant good, as opposed to bad.

Hans nodded. "I'm no good with people. People are people — to me. We all have our different crosses . . . " He stopped, and after a bit I looked over. His lids had settled over his eyes, his back was hunched, his jaw jutted out. His face — pale, with several days' growth — looked like a section of head I had seen in an anatomy lab some years back, in a glass display case filled with formaldehyde.

"Like I said, I can use the work."

Hans's eyes opened, seeming startled by the light that was gradually, inevitably revealing the day. He peered up the mountain. "S'pose you want to sleep."

There were only so many options and I thought — yes — that would be high on my list.

"Been up yet the tree-line road?"

I shook my head.

"Sun it rises twice you know."

"I've seen it from here."

Hans shook his head. "Not the same." His knee began to jerk up and down to some internal beat.

"Same time tonight?"

He didn't answer. I opened the door.

"They throw up four walls and call it a church."

I glanced back.

"They have no ice. Have no rock. They want a church . . . "
He solemnly nodded to the mountain. "They want fire . . . "

"Maybe they don't."

Bones cracked in his neck as he craned his head sideways
without quite looking at me. "May be the case." That said, he
seemed to calm, hiked up his trouser leg and clawed at a spot
on the thickly muscled calf, along which ran a purple scar. It
looked like a mouth, an awful mouth I feared might open
should I stare too long.

Late afternoon I stood before Carl at the hardware store cash
with a coffee percolator.

"Y'know . . . from a certain . . . maybe just the hair."

I noticed Carl checking me over.

"Pete be younger . . . but not that much."

I needed a coffee. I'd slept but not well. My mind was not
yet free of fog.

Carl glanced about the store, shifted his weight, and the
hundred-year-old timber beneath him groaned a response.
The sole other customer was out of hearing. "Hans had a
son. Hans and Greta. Died up the fields. Crevasse. Three
years back."

I'd heard before of such deaths, but at a time when I'd yet
to live near mountains, when the words — the *image* of dropping storeys through ice, of dying wedged in a creeping
mountainside, was somehow abstract.

"Might want to consider a haircut."

Hans came in. He passed on the opposite side of the counter
without looking over, and headed down the aisle to the bulk
supplies.

"That be cash?"

I met Carl's eye, but nothing there suggested anything of what we'd spoken. A whirring, coupled with a sequenced tick, drifted back to us from the rear of the store. Hans was hauling rope off a spool, and looping lengths across his knee. Carl took my money and bagged what I'd bought, circled behind me, and continued down the aisle.

Sometimes I catch myself holding my son in a cradle of arms that feel nearly fused. Something in me wants to believe they'd have to tear my arms from my shoulders in order to remove him, to take him from me. A muscle trembles from my elbow to my wrist, twitch of nerve in my untested flesh. My arms will not be torn from my body. My son will not remain two.

Peter, Hans's son, was an only child, born 1960, twenty when he died, third-year university — this from Carl.

Back in my apartment, I set up the percolator, then realised I still had no coffee. Coming down the stairs at the side of the building I saw Hans loading his burden of rope into the van parked across the street. I stopped and pretended to tie my shoe, my face to the ground, until I heard the engine start and, finally, the van pull away. I stopped back in the hardware store on the pretext of wanting to ask about coffee.

"Use to work nights," said Carl. "In the mine. Ten cups a day it took me to function. Need sedation I tellya if I worked with Hans."

"He's not that hard to work with."

"Oh, not to *work* with." Carl peered out into the dusk settling over the street. "To keep from killin'."

I was twenty-four. Carl was maybe fifty. He'd lived through something — it was anyone's guess — which could give his face a serious menace. His eyes then watered, and softness swept through him.

"Course I never had kids myself." He looked around the store, empty but for us, and cleared his throat. "Time to lock up." His voice was thick. He picked up a box of steel pitons and started back toward the rear. "Wouldn't wait too long," he added, smiling. "Kids . . . they don't grow on trees."

When the van pulled up that night to pick me up, what I noticed first were the two lengths of lumber strapped with bungee cord to the roof. Then I noticed Greta's absence, and took it as a sign of their confidence in me. The fact was she worked as a cook at the Edelweiss Lodge for skiers, and only helped Hans when he was busy or she had days off.

We were drifting in the third quarter-hour of a break which, the night before, had lasted twelve minutes. I felt exclusively aware of the time, and thereby responsible for letting Hans continue. Twice I'd stood — groaned, stretched, sighed — indicating our work awaited. Both times Hans ignored me, set as he was on putting his theology into words.

" . . . alone in the world. Alone till we die, at which time we are stretched out on the rack of His infinitesimal scrutiny, dissected, and judged accordingly. This is why there is so much pain, why there must be — in living — to prepare us. For *then*. Although it does not — how could it? — prepare us. It can only begin to suggest." His glance crept up from the concrete floor and settled on my folded hands. I tried to make sure they did nothing misinterpretable. Hans bolted to his feet. "We can't be held to blame for what happens. We should be held to account for our motives, our intentions, for what we dared to *hope*."

We did mainly business offices that night. Due to the partitions, I didn't see Hans much, but I heard him, a tuneless droning of hymn over the roar of the vacuum. I did the ashtrays, the toilets, the glass, after a while reaching that rhythm to which certain work seems to lend itself. I thought about the interpreter's job, and the odds I might find myself on a trail, on skis, and meet head-on a grizzly bear that could not sleep. It roamed the periphery of my dreams — had since childhood — the beast that wandered beyond good and evil, eater of berries, salmon, men, the largest carnivore walking the earth, the One Fearing Nothing, the hermit god.

Time flew. I found myself done in a half-hour less than the time alloted. I didn't expect any compliments from Hans, I figured more likely suspicions on whether I'd actually done the work. I got neither. Hans vacuumed on, several minutes solid on a spot on the rug I'd have called a stain. We finished the circuit a full hour early, loaded in silence, headed — I thought — toward home. At my intersection Hans didn't pull over. The truck crept through the pulsing orange and on up the slope toward the mountains. He asked did I mind an extra hour's work? I shrugged no, though I don't think it mattered.

Ten minutes later the buckled pavement broke into gravel, ran a few hundred yards, then spread out into a parking loop, beyond which sprawled the glacier. There'd been little snow that year, so manoeuvring was relatively easy, even with the lengths of lumber between us. I'd slung the coil of rope across my shoulder. Hans had on a packsack out of which protruded the handle of a sledge, while behind him he towed a children's sled on which was strapped a large auger, its bit a good nine inches across.

. I was surprised how much one could see — it still being dark — but the sky was clear, we were far enough from trees, and the glacier glowed. Hans either knew his position exact-ly, or did not care, once on the ice. Some fifty yards in and up from the edge, he stopped and we unloaded the supplies. He bored a hole two feet down. We bolted the smaller beam, a four-by-four about seven feet long, across the taller one, a six-by-six twelve feet long — or ten feet, once positioned in the hole. Eye bolts had been screwed into the standing beam on three sides, through which Hans then ran sections of the rope. We hammered pitons into the ice — three, again — on a twenty-foot radius from the beam, and tied on the ropes. We filled the gap around the beam's base with ice shavings from the bore, packed them down with our boots, then backed off. The breeze, gentle for that high up, still sang across the wood and rope. I looked around. Light was drifting over the ridge to the southeast. Another fifty yards above us a dark gap wandered across the ice. I wondered whether this was the one for which he'd been waiting the last three years. Hans was staring up at the cross, rivulets of ice tracing his cheeks.

Word of the cross travelled quickly.

"Won't bring him back," Carl said to me.

"It's something," I countered, feeling a sudden strange pride in that dark morning's work. "Took some doing."

"Shoulda thoughta that before he dragged him out there." Carl paused to pick at a tooth. "Unless he did."

According to Carl, the glacier was slick that day three years back. It was Hans's idea — the climb — to sweat out "poisons" he detected in Peter's thinking since his return from school. They were not properly outfitted in the event of trouble — let alone accident.

"He couldn't have *meant* to . . . " I floundered, "*have* it happen."

Carl drank his coffee. I turned to leave.

"You can't sweat out someone else's poisons."

I turned back, then realized he was not speaking to me. Or not to me alone.

Some weeks later we were sitting on our break — Hans and I — and I was glancing through the paper. We hadn't talked much since the dawn on the slope, part of this due to a cold Hans had caught. Starting mildly enough in his head, it gradually descended and settled in his lungs. The paper had an item on a man in Ontario busted for possession of marijuana. Several joints. The judge in the case called the man "a killer," part of "the Evil" threatening this country, and sentenced him as severely as the law allowed.

I forgot myself — who I was with — and muttered *Christ*, this by chance to the side of Hans's better ear. I noticed him stiffen. "I know the law's the law," I said, "but 'Evil' . . . "

Hans then calmly explained how *assassin* is corrupted from *Hashishin* ("hashish eaters"), an eleventh-century Middle Eastern sect so named for its soldiers being fed hashish prior to their tasks — routinely murders.

"I've never met a dangerous pothead," I told him.

"Evil takes many paths," he said. "Its roots are insidious and far-reaching."

"Marijuana's an opiate. It tranquillizes. It doesn't agitate."

"It kills . . . in the end."

"It might stupefy . . . "

Hans grew paler as we talked, the muscles in his forearms twisting like snakes trying to shed their skin.

"Caught the arsonist did all that damage," he said, holding up another section. "The barns, y'know . . . "

"Yeah. And the cats."

"No mention of cats."

"You know the guy?"

"Know the name. Charged with possession."

"Possession? You said . . . "

"*This* time arson." A thing some people might term a smile flickered briefly over his lips. "Last year possession. This year arson. Got the clipping on file at home. I'll bring it in if you like."

"I trust you." At that moment I also despised him. I thought to ask how long he'd engaged in this hobby, and might've — if not for the cough. It started like a clearing of the throat. Before it was through he was almost doubled over. He straightened up and, without another word, we returned to work.

Greta called the following day to say that Hans had developed pneumonia. They'd let me finish the week alone — if I was willing — but after that, if he wasn't better, they'd contract out. I agreed. They arranged with their clients a reduction of services till Hans was well. Even so, my shifts were extended — eight to eight, with no overtime. The thing though was I could work alone.

Saturday morning finally came. No snow had fallen overnight so the drive up the tree-line road was easy. Just after eight I stood on the glacier midway between the cross and the crevasse. I sucked on a nearly frozen beer. The sun, with little warning, overwhelmed the ridge, met the further side of the ice field, then swept back across it, leaving only thin blue puddles of shadow on the surface. I looked up into a sky so clear that all I could make out were motes adrift on the surface of my eyes. The faintest of chills crept through the stillness, and when I looked down the sun was gone.

For five minutes I barely moved, and then solely to hoist the bottle. I thought about the grizzly. I thought to call its name. I said nothing. Nothing appeared. I don't know how much the glacier moved but gather it must have — it being a glacier. No one can say quite why we're here. The arsonist's lawyer pleaded madness. Valley glaciers I read somewhere can move half a dozen feet a day, continental glaciers ten times that. You try to stand still. You find out it's impossible.

I worked two more months as a janitor, for the outfit that assumed the contracts. I heard from Carl that Hans recovered, but some weeks after I'd left the valley.

The fellow planning the wildlife tour never got it off the ground.

Thinking of the valley, I think most clearly of those few still minutes on the ice that morning. Standing there in the gnawing blue, a heathen, waiting for the sun to return. When it did, it splashed across me like a blessing.

Some hear voices, some act on echoes, others on silence interpreted a hundred ways. All I heard that morning was the wind. Tonight the rattle-throb of the fridge, vehicles drifting down the expressway and, closer, the breathing of my son, his small chest a steady drum on my own.

ROY'S GHOST

None of this woulda likely happened if Roy hadn't went and died. He had his reasons I expect. Not so much he owed me and Calvin money, but just you figure someone would have the decency to tell you they were offing themselves, just so for one thing you don't spend the next couple weeks specting to see them on the street. What Roy did was to all intensive purposes go and let himself die. Sleeping in the open in twenty below. Raincoat and a T-shirt and what they figured as a fatal lack of alcohol in the blood. Now if Roy'd been properly primed, the alcohol woulda functioned as antifreeze and probably by morning they'd of found him still breathing. Maybe got some frostbite, lost a toe or some such thing. But Christ, I mean there's only icycles hanging off of everywhere, and Roy's out back the 7-Eleven in a packing crate in a raincoat with a couple handfuls of that styrofoam they cut up to look like peanuts, well who's he tryna kid. Least we didn't have to see him like that. Blue I expect. Or bluish white. Or grey. Dead at any rate. They got ahold of some sister or cousin from someplace like Moose Jaw or Medicine Hat. I been through there on a Greyhound must be twenty years ago or so, it was Hallowe'en or Remembrance Day and all you could see was stiff dirt and sky like bad news going on and on and on like your basic no-tomorrow. Holy jumpin', I mean really. You can just imagine this person, this lady used to prairie winters thinking Christ Almighty freezing to death on the streets of Toronto? Yeah well it's not the first time.

First time for Roy of course but he wasn't setting any presidents.

We'd been living in this pisshole as it were, first me, then Calvin and me, then Calvin and me and occasionally Roy, specially in lousy weather. It suited our needs. We weren't on too bad terms with the management cept for this once we nearly got the boot for Roy raising a stink when he found out we were signing over the welfare to the landlord. We were getting money back for our basic requirements, but Roy seemed to think this was poor financial planning. Thing was, I was bringing in in the range of two-hunnerd-seventeen a month, rent was two-thirty-five, and I don't care how good you are at math, it's some feat to survive on minus eighteen dollars a month. So that's how Calvin moved in. Roy we just run into at the mission a lot. He was fairly malnutreated so we figured let's be good smaritans.

So this one night we were all fairly buzzed and the talk got around to life in general, experiences, and that sort of thing. And I told about meeting some FLQ guys in Trois Rivières in '69 or '70, hitching through, and they picked me up and I still had some semblance of high school French so we got on okay. I always liked French people. The thing was though these guys had guns. A whole trunkful. I don't know why they told me but it made an impression. So that was fine, I told my story, then Calvin spouted off some complicated bullshit about being related to Louis Riel as a matter of fact, and having dreams of being hung and sometimes having entire dreams in some Métis language he can't remember a word of when he wakes up. And the longer he talked the more I got the sense that Calvin thought he was the reincarnation of Louis Riel. Which is fine if that's what you want to believe. But Christ, if I was Riel I wouldn't want to know I'd come back to earth as Calvin. Anyhow, that left Roy. Roy musta sat there a full minute, like he was tryna decide whether not his story was worth it.

Roy's story was this: he'd been dead. Five or six minutes, after some kind of accident. They thought he was a goner but managed to revive him. When he came to he noticed his ambition was gone, and nothing in the world could bring it back. He'd got too relaxed. Now normally we woulda laughed in his face, but something in the way he sat there like it didn't matter whether not we believed him made me for one believe him. Calvin wasn't sure. More like he was pissed off cause Roy had come up with such a simple amazing story. But Calvin wasn't gonna let it rest till he got some concrete details on what being dead was like. All Roy said was: *beige, with a hum.*

Beige, with a hum. Well Calvin coulda screamed. He was so frustrated with Roy's little story he threatened to knock his block off. But Roy just sat there picking at his teeth, then after a moment raised his head. *Oh yeah*, he said, *and a smell like a blown fuse.* This time Calvin coulda gone through the ceiling. He stormed about the room like a tornado that couldn't make up its mind what to destroy. He finally grabbed up his coat, told Roy Roy'd better get the hell out, then left. Roy finished up his teeth and began to gather up his things. He smiled in a specially sad sort of way, a way that sured me he'd been telling the truth, the truth to the best of his ability. After that night I saw him once maybe twice more times, but he never said much. The smile was still there, only bigger, worse. The smile had moved off to both sides of his face, moving like a zipper around his head till finally the upper half would have to fall off. I knew it. I knew it, but what can you say?

Now I been depressed far back as I remember, though I never got around to doing myself in. Partly since if you're brung up Catholic it's the one sin they're never gonna let you live down. So what I'm tryna establish here, what I think is important to note, is that what followed, the circumstances, the sequence of events, per say, was not a case of me tryna follow Roy's footsteps.

This one night just after supper maybe a week or so after the news on Roy, Calvin comes in holding of all things a weejeeboard he'd found in the garbage. It still looked usable, though it's hard to tell when something like a weejeeboard's still usable. *Only know by trying*, goes Calvin. His plan of course was to try and go and scare up old Roy. I had my qualms. Roy was a nice enough fella and all but death can do strange things to people. But Calvin insisted and his weakest argument wasn't the forty-ouncer of CC he'd picked up for the occasion. *Gotta get calm and receptive*, goes Calvin, and he got no argument from me on that score. So pretty soon it's getting up towards nine o'clock and the band downstairs is starting up, which is a bit distracting but Calvin says it's okay it'll just cover over the noise of Roy returning from wherever, which Calvin figured might get pretty loud. My heart gives a funny jump but I guessed it was just my medication smacking into the booze in my bloodstream. I got a bad heart so I try not to mix too much, but I'm doing my part to get calm and receptive. I suddenly have to take a leak so I make the expedition down the hall to the can and luckily there's no lineup or other aggravation and I'm there taking a leisurely leak and I reach down to shake myself off. I reach down to shake myself off and I swear it feels like a corpse's fingers fiddling with my dick. I look down to make sure the fingers are mine, and they are, but cold. Like someone else's. Anyhow I make it back and we just keep throwing back the rye and we must be nearly two-thirds through when over the traffic and the band downstairs and the waterpipes and the mice in the walls we make out a tiny knock. A tiny tiny tiny knock. On our door. Now I start thinking holy jeez we haven't done a seance or nothing and man is it possible we *willed* him back? And I start tryna member if there's anything I ever said to Roy that could give him just cause to do me in and I can't think and before you can even begin to say boo old Calvin like some halfwit victim in any one of a million movies I'm trying like mad to *not* remember gets up walks over and throws the door wide open. Ends up it's just some character from down the hall who wants to know if we got some smokes to spare, and I'm so relieved I spose not being quite receptive enough for ghosts yet I start feeding the joker half my pack of Players till Calvin has to grab my hand to make me stop.

So that gets rid of some excess tension. Once we're back into a reasonable state of calm, Calvin looks over to the wee-jeeboard and starts going on about once as a kid when he and some friends tried to bring back Winston Churchill. Churchill never came but they got some neat wind and supposedly the name of the girl Calvin would marry. It didn't work out that way and I made the mistake of asking why, which brought us to the issue of Calvin's ex-wife Claire, and how if he'd been in his right mind he'd of strangled her when he had the chance, and so on and so on with that sort of sentiment. When Calvin gets going he's hard to stop, so I just laid back and stared at the nude Madonna pictures he'd tacked up on his side of the room. And it musta occurred to me I wasn't feeling all that well, but Calvin's voice kept on and on driving me downward into sleep. Next thing I know I'm waking in Emergency, plugged into all sorts of gadgets and devices. I got this memory this sense of something familiar but can't put my finger on it. Now I got a pretty inquiresome mind so I turn to the attendant and ask what gives. He turns to me and starts beaming like a headlight, like I'm some lost relative or winning number. As it happens I'm in for a shock. My sources inform me I was dead a couple minutes. Calvin had been good enough to stop his story when I stopped breathing, he'd run downstairs and found an ambulance — passing — with nothing on the agenda. Now that strikes me like serious coincidence. Furthermore, I never been treated so nicely in that hospital before. Everybody tryna shake my hand. Everybody tryna be my best friend. And Calvin sitting there only starting to get some colour back in his face. For a moment I figured I musta missed out, that Roy musta come and gone while I was out. But it's just the excitement had gotten to Calvin, and the only thing he wanted to know, once we'd gotten a minute to talk, was what being dead was like.

Now this is the funniest part to me personally, the part the guy from the book on dying and coming back to life will pay cash for. This is the part that's getting me free coffees so long as I'm a client of the mission. I swear they treat me like a saint down there now. Used to be, before I died, they'd hardly touch me with a ten-foot pole. But times change and do they ever. Thing that kills me most is this: Roy was basically telling the truth. Being dead *is* beige — a kind of bright beige you don't witness often, but beige, with a sort of air conditioner hum. I'm still not good with your basic pain, but death, with death it's another story. I can think of worse ways to spend your time.

COMMON SENSE ■

A man, a drink or so shy of brimming, was trying to mount an unstable chair. The bouncer had his back to him, but not Pearl, she couldn't look away. The TV's colour had gone all haywire and the man with the chair was intending to fix it. Not that it mattered to most in the room, the Leafs were blowing another lead. A haggard blonde woman with black roots yelled something to the man, he paid her no attention, she knocked over her draft glass, then went back to smoking. In the far other corner a pubescent band was bombarding the drinkers too drunk to move. Pearl moved her arm but her sleeve stuck to a shiny flat patch on the terry cloth tablecloth where long ago some elbow had melted. She kept on watching the balancing act. You couldn't call it an act exactly, Pearl well knew, the man was an innocent, he'd taken hold of the room by accident, other heads now turning his way.

While Cecil had been off getting smokes, Pearl had had that feeling again, of losing it, of her self disappearing, while something numb and bent replaced it. The moment passed, as usual, yet left in its wake a lingering façade infecting everything around her. But the man working his way off the ground, negotiating those first crucial feet, reassured her and made her feel real. Human and normal, with the hint of a buzz. Someone scored but you couldn't tell who. The man rose up, as if on the applause, and his finger reached the dial. The bouncer wasn't new to the scene, he was there in a second, his own hand rose up, took the man by the scruff of the neck and hauled him to the floor. Cecil, facing the other way, missed the encounter but spotted the waiter and signalled for another round.

Cecil worked with the bass player's brother, who'd assured him they'd get in without cover charge. "Just say you're friends of Max's brother. Max the Axeman. You'll get the royal treatment." As it turned out there wasn't a cover, it was Wednesday after all, and the band was unknown. Cecil drove cab and routinely dropped by a health food restaurant in which Pearl worked. They'd got to talking, he always looked so awkward, falafel and hot sauce always to go. Coffee double double, it never varied, standing at the cash like he dreaded being seen. They'd met at a movie, then a second. This was the first thing resembling a date.

Pearl winced at a blast of feedback, then reached for another in a stream of cigarettes. "Never accept ideas from strangers," said Cecil, but his comment got lost in the din. Cupping her ear, Pearl leaned forward. It was the sort of tossed-off comment he hated to have to repeat, if she heard it she heard it, if she didn't — fine. He looked at her ear. As ears go it was pretty nice. Every now and then Cecil had these flashes: how stupid ears looked, or nostrils, or eyebrows. Anyone's, it didn't matter. So under the circumstances Pearl's was fine. He repeated his comment, then added a shrug. Pearl smiled, raised her hand like a pistol, grimaced and pretended to blow her brains out. Cecil laughed, they both did. The band continued its sonic assault and not too much later they found themselves dancing. They danced on and off till last call, like neither one of them had in years.

"Live and learn," said Cecil as they left the bar with the last of the patrons. The Leafs had hung on to tie 6-6, the band had somehow engineered an encore, no blood had been spilled, and everyone could walk.

"No, it was fun," Pearl said as she undid the lock on her bike and then worked the rusty chain around the seat-post.

"They got those . . . what are they . . . " The word escaped him. "You know, like in Superman."

"Kryptonite."

"Yeah, yeah, kryptonite locks."

"Yeah, but they cost more than the bike."

Cecil nodded. He scratched his chin. His chin was okay, it did its job. They stood looking off in opposite directions, pretending to enjoy the fresh spring air so far untainted by the rendering plants. Cecil was trying his best not to blow it. Pearl was worried about her body language. She wanted to come across as friendly and cool and sensuous, but not up-tight or sleazy. Cecil was waiting for the right words to come. A train meanwhile made all this cold lonesome night noise, keening and cracking its bones in the Junction. Cecil and Pearl watched their pupils dilate.

"Hey, y'play cards?" Cecil ventured.

"I have, I mean . . . "

"I don't know, I just figured you don't have to work to-morrow and I'm not scheduled till graveyards startin' Friday and seeing Wanda'll probably be up still . . . euchre, I don't know, or rummy, how 'bout it?"

Pearl considered. Wanda was his mother. Most guys at thirty didn't still live with their mothers, but as he explained it his father had died a long while back, Cecil had come and gone over the years, there weren't other kids, they got on okay, they split expenses just like friends would.

"Sure, why not," she said, trying to sound enthused. Other options weren't knocking down the door. Cecil's or a donut shop, or head home alone. Not that she couldn't ask him back to her place, but she wouldn't, and she wasn't sure why. He was nice. Too nice for a one-night stand. His place she could leave, he lived with his mother, whereas she wasn't sure she could send him home from hers. She'd think about it sober. Besides, cards were fun.

Several hands into some animated rummy, Pearl voiced the suspicion she was out of her league.

"Nonsense," said Wanda, who led by a hundred points. She reached forward to take a card. As she did, her sleeve rode up her arm, exposing from just past the wrist to the elbow a tartan of scar, old but indelible. Pearl got a shiver at the thought of each cut.

"So you wanna marry my son," said Wanda.

Pearl smiled back with complete incomprehension.

Wanda coughed then lay down two full runs of face cards.

"First," said Cecil, "she ruins your concentration. If that doesn't work, she cheats."

Wanda sucked on her cigarette, then squinted through the out-going smoke.

"Moms don't cheat," she said. "Moms are holy. Get that through your head, my son." She caught Pearl's eye with a sad look. "He's got some things to learn yet."

"Huh," said Cecil, as though his throat were clogged.

Pearl didn't know quite what to think. Whenever she witnessed families get along, regardless of the banality, it made her morose. To sit at a table and disagree without things spiralling out of control, to spend time together and enjoy each other's company without getting wounded or needing to wound. She looked up from her accumulating cards to Cecil's gentle touch on her arm. Neither beer nor ruminating usually made her cry, but combined they sometimes had this effect.

"Sorry," she said. "My play I guess." She wiped her eyes but things remained blurry.

"You okay?" asked Cecil.

Pearl wiped her eyes again, this time managing to trail eyeliner out from the socket and almost to the ear. "It's just . . . it's when . . . when I see people . . . "

Wanda glanced at the smeared eye, looked down but failed to stifle a snort. She took a tissue from her sweater sleeve and wiped the chaos from Pearl's face. "There's lots of good reasons," Wanda assured her.

"It's weird, y'know," said Pearl. "Seeing people get along, people related who still get along." She considered this, coughed, then had a sip of beer.

Wanda and Cecil exchanged looks.

"Wasn't so chummy when Vern was around, rest in peace and so on," said Wanda.

A silence which might be construed as respectful but was in fact accidental ensued. Cecil drank. Pearl took out a cigarette, paused, then put it back. Wanda contemplated her cards without much enthusiasm.

"How 'bout," said Wanda, "we pick this game up later. Probably I oughta be getting to bed." She got up from the table and recapped her beer. "I'm glad to've met you." She took Pearl's hand and held it a moment. "If you ever need to talk . . . "

"Thanks," said Pearl.

"I mean it," said Wanda.

"She means it," said Cecil. "She may cheat but she doesn't lie."

They said their good-nights and Wanda left the room. Cecil went to get himself another beer. After a minute a faint sound

rose from down the hall, an eerie human droning of erratic
pitch. Pearl was staring wide-eyed when Cecil returned.

"Just a record she got from the library. Inuit folk songs.
She says it helps to stimulate her dreams."

"Christ, I guess so."

"She writes them down. They're really something," he said
with some pride. Pearl liked the idea. "It's cheap," said Cecil.
"It's cheap entertainment." He found himself caught between
praise and explanation.

"Oh yeah," Pearl said to put him at his ease.

The music droned on. She felt herself drifting, and decided
it was time to go. Cecil wanted to call her a cab.

"I got my bike."

"Y'ride home at this hour?"

"Safest time. The roads're deserted."

Cecil insisted on escorting her to the curb. They kissed
cheeks, then there was a moment neither of them knew quite
what to do with. Cecil finally reached across and patted her
arm. They agreed to see each other soon. Pearl pedalled off,
and soon was gone in fog. Cecil went back upstairs.

He felt okay. In fact he felt good. But he'd pay for the
beers if he didn't sober up a bit. He got out the chessboard
and had a quick game. He sensed he was being preferential to
White, so abandoned the game when Black lost its queen.
Evangelists were all that was left on TV. He watched with the
sound off for some vague time. The aching faces. He couldn't
read their lips. Gradually sleep overtook him.

Standing against the viaduct railing, her bike on its side, Pearl
peered down at the black creeping river. In all directions the
city slept, the peace was mammoth, a low drugged throb. She
knew the fall alone wouldn't kill her, instinct would inter-

vene and make the entrance knifelike. If it came to that. And, a strong swimmer, she count not could on panicked floundering once in the water. She caught a whiff of the rich stench rising from the fluid below. She had second thoughts. Death should not be disgusting. Meaning, of course, if one had the choice.

She remembered a certain muskrat carcass which, as a kid with a couple of friends, she'd discovered in the creek behind their house during spring melt. Turning the swollen sack with a stick to poke at the tangle of jellied organs, the kids then chased each other around with *the stick that turned the muskrat over*, at once intrigued and repulsed by the thought of being so close to *contamination*. After all it wasn't death they'd been so sternly warned against, but dead things, and what they carried. They finally pushed the carcass back out to continue downstream in its soggy decay. Again she considered the river below. Rats might survive, but not much else.

Oblivious to the car's first passing, she only looked up when it circled back and came to a screeching stop beside her.

"Hey baby, wanna sit on my face?" the man in the passenger seat inquired.

This sort of question always threw Pearl. If she sat on his face would he finally find peace? satiation? companionship? She took a closer look at the man, who wasn't so much a man as a boy, sixteen or seventeen but well-built, not plagued with the pimples of his back-seat friends, but just as wired, which gave him the courage.

"Thanks," said Pearl, "but I got a toilet at home." The comment sounded okay in her head but vocalised was another matter.

"Is that right, cunt," the kid replied, then struggled with his low-slung door. No sooner was it open than it jammed on the elevated curb. A beer bottle fell out and broke in the gutter.

"Watch the fuckin' door," said the driver.

Pearl climbed up onto the bridge railing, balancing herself with an arm around a lamp pole. She figured number one would get a boot to the head, but after that it might be swan-dive city. The kid had worked his way partly out when a hubbub rose amongst the others. Looking up he met Pearl's fierce, unsubmitting glare. He stopped, almost as if to won-der what it was he was planning to do. A hand reached out from the back seat, grabbed him by the belt, and pulled him back in. Down the street a police car had appeared. The kid closed his door, then started to laugh. With a laying of rubber the car took off. Pearl stayed put. It wasn't essential. But sometimes you have to savour the moment. She glanced again at the uninviting water. The cops had stopped and were asking her questions. Blood was buzzing in her ears. She knew she was alive, but why tell them? She knew who she was, but why tell them?

She'd been in a psychiatric hospital before, but not since age eight when she'd gone to see her father. To arrive as a patient was something else. Pearl might have managed to talk the cops out of it, claim she was drunk or had been threatened and so forth. But something prevented her, she felt like a spectator watching the handling of someone else. Words seemed premature, words would maybe ruin things.

The time when she was eight she'd managed to get lost in the seemingly labyrinthine halls. She'd been rescued by a woman who found everything funny. A mouth like a beat-up piano keyboard. The most unhappy laugh she'd heard. And the woman's firm assertion that Pearl's father was hopelessly intelligent, and this constituted his only problem. Her father had sat there looking sadder than ever. A man beside him was shouting out chess moves — *Get the king before he castles! Get the king or you'll regret it*! Pearl's father ignored the man, turned to Pearl and brought her close. The moist stubble scraped against her cheek, he stank of sweat, he quivered.

The doctor asked Pearl if she wanted to harm herself. Pearl confessed that she didn't really know. It probably depended on what he meant by *harm*. But no, she had no concrete plans.

Did she want to harm others?

Pearl looked down at the man's tanned feet, his clogs, his ashram pants, his Rolex.

"There are people I have no use for," said Pearl.

The doctor made a note.

Pearl's two new roommates were Joan, cocooned in sheets, and Rita, surly and rigid, sitting smoking on her bed. A nurse, alerted by undispersed smoke rings, directed her to the lounge.

"You plan on slashing," Rita monotoned, "keep the blood off my bed, okay? Other people's blood really grosses me out." She elegantly flicked an ash and proceeded past them down the hall.

Pearl was checked for any sharp objects, was given a physical, pyjamas, a toothbrush, and strong encouragement to get some sleep. She wasn't tired, in spite of the beers, so decided to take a wander through the unit. Magic-markered posters outlined various stress-management techniques. Schedules set out the unit routine. In the doorway of one room a staff person sat facing a patient strapped to a bed. Both were asleep, which somehow pleased Pearl. She continued around till she came to the patients' lounge, wherein Rita sat, curled up, rolling a cigarette. Fish persisted in a tiny aquarium. Pearl hadn't seen live fish close up in years, so bent down to study them.

"Y'hungry?" asked Rita. "We could fry a couple up."

Pearl ignored her.

"Most excitement the things've had in months. They're particularly keen on people coming up and mashing their faces against the glass, all that skin oil and crud and lipstick smeared right across their only window on the world. Fun times." She dragged a gummy tongue down the rolling paper's edge. "Or we could always feed 'em to death. That's always good for a laugh."

"You got your room back," said Pearl without turning.

"Fuck you too," said Rita matter-of-factly.

Pearl didn't even bother to think. She got up, walked over, and stood in front of Rita. "Listen . . . " she started, but words wouldn't come. She then had a thought about a blunt object.

"Wanna smoke?" Rita asked vaguely, thrusting forth her pouch of tobacco. "We gotta look out for each other y'know. Me an' you, shit, we're pretty near likely the only sanely remote ones around."

Remote. That was it, what Pearl was feeling. She sat on the couch and let it sink in.

Rita moved over. "My time is your time, my tobacco's your tobacco, just say the word." She threw her arm over Pearl's shoulder and gave her a solid, cradling hug.

Pearl relaxed and felt the floodgates open.

Cecil woke to the phone call the following day. Wanda was out, and things were slow to register. Pearl said at first she just wanted to talk, but then she revealed her circumstances. Cecil said sure that he'd come visit, he had to get his head on straight, but then he'd be in. Pearl said not to worry, it was strange but not urgent. She was fine but locked up, she'd explain it more later.

When he got to the hospital Pearl was being seen, but they invited him to wait in the patients' lounge. The soaps were on and two men sat watching. They wore street clothes and were drinking what appeared to be coffee from tooth-marked styrofoam cups. Cecil couldn't tell if they were patients or guests, so sat back and tried to go unnoticed.

"Should see this one place," said one of the men. "They come out and dance right over you."

"Y'mean with the glass ledge you sit sorta under?"

"No . . . " said the first, wincing with impatience. "Place I'm talkin they got those . . . whataya call 'em . . . fuck, I'm drawin' a blank . . . The girls come out right onto the tables, they got the tables bolted, like. They even got these heel-hole deals for the chick's shoes so she don't slip and fall if the table's wet or something? These chicks, I'm tellinya, they squat right down. Might as well dip the old muff right in. You pay extra, I don't know, a couple bucks, but what the hell."

"Good angle, eh."

"*Good angle*, he says! She's like *that*!" He mimed out a boomerang of flesh dangling round about forehead level.

"And dances?"

"Wudja need dancin' for, it's starin' you in the face."

They considered this.

"She's out of being seen if you want to follow me," said a nurse to Cecil from the lounge doorway.

Pearl was sitting at the end of Rita's bed, with Rita at the head, Rita's knees pulled up under an over-size sweater. The lump called Joan remained where she'd been twelve hours earlier upon Pearl's admission. The nurse went over and attempted to rouse her, with little or no success.

"She's breathing," said Rita. "I checked her earlier. Pulse is okay but she's starting to smell."

The nurse acknowledged Rita with a warning smile.

Cecil explained he could only stay briefly but then he'd be back in a couple of hours. "So how's it goin' anyway?"

"Okay," said Pearl. "Could be worse. They coulda certified me."

"Certified you what?"

Pearl glanced at the nurse. "A risk to myself . . . or a risk to a doctor."

The nurse gave up on Joan and left.

"Least," said Rita, "it's not like mid-evil times. Back then, you mouth off, you *look* at some creep the wrong way you land up burnt at the stake." From underneath her sweater, with the altered message — CHOOSE LIFE *BOATS* — she pulled out an ashtray and a lit cigarette.

Pearl introduced them.

"Can I be frank?" asked Rita.

Cecil could think of no reason why not.

"We're dealing," she said, "with a fundamental clash of belief systems. I'm here, I'm a twentieth-century woman. A late late *very* late twentieth-century woman. I'm not a rabbit for Revlon, okay?" She aimed her huge black eyes at Cecil's, crossed her spindly arms, and suctioned the last life off her cigarette. "Why did the manic enter the hospital?" She peered back and forth from one to the other. "No takers? I'll tellya. No big surprise: so she'd get properly nailed to the cross." She sighed and took out another cigarette. "Y'see, most manics got this thing for martyrdom. Odd thing with me's I hate the stuff, I had saints stuffed up my nose since squirthood. I'm going through the motions, you see what I'm saying? They push it though, they keep me here much longer, I *am* gonna goddam metamorphosize, they want a saint they'll get a saint, likes of which those pecker-track jerk-offs have not witnessed in a thousand years. Good thing too. It's been dull around here."

A thin, sickly, dishevelled man appeared at the door, grinning.

"Mark," said Rita, "how goes the battle?"

"I took Joe's Aqua Velva challenge," said Mark. "I lost. I'm the underdog. Y'got a cigarette?"

Pearl offered one from some Cecil had brought her.

"Piss me off I end up puking," said Mark, without removing the grin.

"You puke in my room you'll clean it with your face," said Rita. She sprang from the bed and met him at the door, took him by his clothes-hanger collarbone and led him off down the hall.

"Fun bunch," said Cecil.

"Yeah," said Pearl, "considering."

Cecil followed Pearl's glance toward the lump called Joan.

Wanda was at a loss. She'd got home late and heard Cecil's message, that Pearl was in hospital, the psychiatric unit, she was okay but being kept for observation, he'd call again when he got a chance. Visiting hours were over at nine and Wanda didn't get the news till almost eight. For the next hour she'd been struggling with a note, to buoy Pearl's spirits, to assure her that times like these could be gotten through. But what annoyed her was she'd been in Pearl's position, even worse, and *she could talk*. It didn't seem, however, she could make it sensible. She studied her arms where they lay on the table, like relics, like someone else's limbs. And above the scars the tiny tattoo, a purple ensign with the words *common sense* — her god when all else had failed. Simple words to dissuade the razor, to rob the knife of its cheap appeal. She looked once more at the scribbled letter which tried to tell Pearl of the joke of it all, there was so much time to become dead, there wasn't a rush, it would come with time. You had to see the joke involved, the patience needed to laugh it off.

But Wanda wasn't laughing it off. She was sipping sherry at a reckless pace. Her eyes felt raw, and stung with any contact with the lids. Pearl reminded her too much of herself, with a sadness anchored unfathomably deep. If the world was a disappointment to Pearl, then the world would have to be changed.

She sealed the note with a kiss, and sat back. She was hopeful. She didn't want to dwell on it, but she realized she'd forgotten how much hope she could contain.

The Leafs were trailing by three at the end of the first when visiting hours ended. The P.A. announcement came harsh and staccato, jarring from stasis all but Mark and Rita.

"Woman's on speed," someone muttered.

Mark, having emptied his system of its contents, was deep in a corner grunting to his Walkman. Rita had been calmed down. She was calm now, she didn't even blink.

"Who knows?" said Cecil, regarding the game. "Maybe they'll come out strong in the second." No one challenged him on this opinion. He got up and made his way into his coat.

"Never know, do you," said Pearl, regarding many things.

"You never do," Cecil confirmed.

"Say hi to Wanda . . . "

"If there's anything you need . . . "

"When I got it figured out . . . "

She saw him to the door. He wished her the best, and gave her an awkward but certain kiss, on the cheek but very close to the lips, in front of a nurse who was holding open the door.

Back in the lounge, Pearl picked up the paper. She came across an article she'd missed the first time through. It described a study, recently completed, which concluded that being a woman in this country constituted a risk to one's mental health. *No kidding*, she said to herself, but it did surprise her at some level, to find something she'd felt instinctively for years get acknowledged in the mainstream press. She glanced around the room but the numbers were even, men to women, even so. She peered about through the dense tobacco veils, the flickering barrage from the TV suspended several feet above their heads, through phantom conversations still hanging in the air, wasted breaths, mutilated auras, let alone electron swarms from Saturn, who killed his children, who *devoured his children* . . . and Rita's stony profile came into focus.

Pearl tore out the article and went to find her nurse.

Wanda was listening to Celtic chants when Cecil wandered in.

"Think the house was haunted," he said.

"Every house is haunted," said Wanda. "So . . . how's she faring?"

Cecil gave the workings of a shrug, sat down, got back up, took off his coat, and went to the kitchen.

"You saw her," said Wanda, assuming that much.

"Yeah." Cecil came back, a beer in hand. "I don't know." He took a gulp, sat down, and gently clawed at the label. "I sat there like an idiot. I didn't know what to say. She's there in this room . . . " He looked at Wanda, couldn't continue, and looked at the floor.

"At least you were there. That's the important thing."

"Is it?"

Wanda gave a blank look. Could she even remember the important thing? If, back then, another person helped, or kind words, or flowers. If kisses got you anywhere through it, or threats, or guilt, or chocolates. Vern, she recalled, had let her know he hadn't a clue what her problem was, he'd leave it to the doctors, she'd have to trust the doctors, but he wouldn't desert her if that was her worry. What he meant was he wouldn't run out, he'd keep living in their house with her, which is what he did.

Blankets, those had been important. Hearing the wind in the trees outside. Clocks, by comparison, had been a joke. *Tomorrow's another day* meant nothing once the concept of day, tomorrow or otherwise, lost the better part of its meaning. She'd dreamt of a baby, decided she was holy, a Madonna, carrying God within her. Wanda hadn't, prior to that, given much thought to herself as a person. Other people were obviously persons, but with herself it didn't seem so obvious. Still, she thought she could *raise* a person. So after the holiness had run its course she set her mind on being a mother. She'd got Vern involved, and Cecil came about. She realized there wasn't one important thing, the thing was a process, you had to ride it out.

"Time'll tell, I guess," said Cecil, then reached forward and turned on the TV.

Wanda went and stood by the window, faintly swaying from side to side.

The Leafs scored but Cecil hardly noticed. He'd played, he wasn't a stranger to the game, he had a broken nose from a cross-check. Tonight, though, the game didn't have any impact. Skates were pretty funny if you really took a look at them. The Celtic chants continued, they were weird but not unbearable. He hadn't asked Wanda if they were religious, but they felt religious, in a way he could stomach.

The record ended, and Cecil got up and went to the kitchen to make a sandwich. He heard the record start again, it sounded like the same side, but with that kind of music it was hard to tell. The sandwich took on a life of its own, tottering up like the Tower of Babel. It took some doing to get it in one hand. He leaned against the fridge and ate the sandwich, carefully bringing it up to his face, then bringing it back to the plate, smaller. You have to eat, or you disappear. Still, it should've had more taste.

"Son of a gun!" It was Wanda's voice. He was used to her mood swings, even so, he leaned from the kitchen to have a look. Pearl stood just inside the door, Wanda wrapped in welcome around her.

"Wha'd you . . . *escape*?" said Wanda.

"I signed out, 'Against Medical Advice.' I had to sign a form so they don't get held responsible."

"As if they ever were!" said Wanda.

Cecil came forward, trying to chew clear a passage sufficient for speech.

In taking her coat off, Pearl turned, and a fluid suction noise rose from her foot. "Got a soaker. These boats've had it."

"Get those socks off," Wanda directed, then went off down the hall to get some dry ones.

"So, I mean . . . y'can just stroll out?" Cecil said, impressed.

"Well, it's kind of funny." Pearl accepted a sip from the beer he held out. "I was sitting there in front of this TV, this room full of people facing this TV, the room we were in."

Cecil nodded.

"It's like, y'know, I've never had a TV. I don't mean they're evil. Just they never seemed that crucial."

Cecil nodded.

"So there I was, this room with this TV. The TV Room they call it. And we're all there watching. The program wasn't even all that stupid. It just got me wondering what I was doing there."

"Yeah. Hmmmm." He swigged his beer.

The Leafs scored to tie the game, and both of them turned to watch the replay. Cecil was the first to look away, but Pearl kept watching so he looked back.

"There's no way," said Pearl, her eyes a little glassy.

"Sorry?"

Pearl's gaze finally broke from the screen. She smiled and took out a cigarette. "One of the doctors? I seen him in the restaurant, he comes in all the time, tips like shit. They're gonna have a hoot when they hear what he does." Pearl's smile quickly dissolved.

Wanda returned with an armful of socks.

"One's plenty," Pearl said.

"Most people like to choose," said Wanda. "But I'll say one thing concerning hospitals. When I went into hospital I couldn't play Fish to save my life. I couldn't believe what I'd been missing."

As Pearl leaned forward to pull on the socks, she noticed the rummy game laid out as they'd left it.

"Your play," said Wanda, "if memory serves."

Cecil was grinning to wet his pants.

"As for you, my son, while you're up, be so good as ta bring us a beer?"

Wanda looked from Cecil to Pearl. She didn't want to get any notions. Enough they were here with her, people she could talk to. Enough she hadn't looked at their cards, she'd resisted temptation, and held out hope. She might have said a prayer of thanks, had it been in her nature. Instead, she just sat there in the middle of that moment, feeling quite positive, given the world.

ACKNOWLEDGEMENTS

The following stories have been previously published, some in slightly different forms, in the following magazines and anthologies:

"Roy's Ghost" in *The Malahat Review*, No. 84, 1988.

"South of Here" in *The Fiddlehead*, No. 163, 1990.

"Common Sense" in *The Malahat Review*, No. 92, 1990; *The Journey Prize Anthology – 3* (Toronto: McClelland & Stewart, 1991).

"Zieman Besieged" in *Matrix*, No. 32, 1991.

"Towards Deirdre's" in *IslandSide*, November 1991; winner of the Carl Sentner Award for Short Fiction, 1991.

"Sea of Tranquility" in *The New Quarterly*, Vol. 12, No. 3, 1993.

"Cerberus" in *Grain*, Vol. 20, No. 4, 1992.

"The Siutation What It Does to Him Personally" in *Event*, Vol. 22, No. 1, 1993.

"Omens" in PRISM *International*, Vol. 31, No. 2, 1993.

"Vacuums" in *The Malahat Review*, No. 102, 1993

"Nickel & Dime" in *The Fiddlehead*, No. 176, 1993.